Buried
TREASURE

Printed in Australia
First Printing 2025
ISBN: 978-1-7636899-0-9
White Light Publishing
whitelightuniversal.com.au

Acknowledgements

As an avid reader I get to read lots of acknowledgements, and I am often blown away by how seemingly long some are that it can feel like an extra short story. It's always interesting to see what help is involved in producing the finished product and what experts in their fields were consulted. Along with the research involved.

But can assure you this won't be close to being a short story. Though not short of my heartfelt thanks.

For many years I have been heard to repeat the words of the mystic Meister Eckhart

"The greatest prayer that can ever be said is thank you."

So, what follows is my prayer of thanks.

Firstly, thank you to Julia Van Der Sluys and White Light publishing. Julia is publisher, editor and cheer squad all rolled into one. She is a true Lightworker.

Thank you to Kirstin Lopdell for creating Buried Treasure's beautiful cover. And of course, how the book would appear between the covers. I only needed to share what I was picturing in my mind's eye and there it was. Got to love synchronicity at work when that occurs.

Thank you, Crow, otherwise known as Black Crow Walking. She was happy for me to use her name in Buried Treasure. And she really does run Angelic Retreats at the Old Monastery, Stroud NSW. Which is where Stella and Cassie meet. Johanna is one of my sisters in law and I have faithfully quoted her words. Thank you, see I do listen to what you say.

Thank you to all those who have walked in and out of the chapters of my own life book. Whatever your role in any of those pages, whether it felt not so good at the time or wonderful. I am grateful always for the opportunity to heal what I needed to heal and to evolve and awaken to loving me as me. I send you love.

Thank you to my friends, you know who you are, and family who encourage me to continue my author journey. Your belief in me never fails to move me and I carry you all in my heart.

Haven't run out of prayers yet. Thank you to my husband Brian, who is my biggest fan and encourages me to use my wings to fly. One might say he is the man behind the woman.

If you are still reading and if this hasn't turned into a short story, I thank you, the reader.

To you all I send love from my heart to yours and the biggest smile I can muster.

May you always choose Joy.

Patricia Lovell

The Mountain Top

I sit on the mountain top
Alone and unafraid.
Gazing into oneness
And in the clear view
I am finally seeing me .
As part of this oneness
Part of all I see.
And no longer worried
About being me.
Only wanting to simply be.

The struggle to the mountain top,
Has been hard and often
I've been tired.
And even now as I experience
The mountain top.
I see the valleys below.
Which still may beckon me.

But in the knowing and
The dreaming .
I know I've made it
To the mountain top.
And there I can always be.
For from a valley
There's another mountain to climb
Where I can simply be.

November 1988

This work is dedicated to those who are willing, to pause a moment and choose their own path.

The one they will enjoy.

"A dream you dream alone is only a dream.
A dream you dream together is reality."

John Lennon

CASSIE

On the Road

It was such a relief to leave the busy motor way that matched the hectic rush of their morning. The countryside they were now driving through was such a contrast that Cassie noticed her frayed nerves around getting away on time being soothed. It was a bonus that the morning drizzle and looming grey clouds had given way to a clear blue sky and glorious sunshine. Glancing at her husband there appeared to be a lessening of the strain that in recent times had been etched on his face so she thought Josh must be feeling something similar.

Her thoughts were confirmed as Josh's comments broke into her thoughts. "If we get nothing else out of this Angelic retreat, we will have had a change of pace along with the sense of calm that simply driving through these vivid green fields and rolling hills creates." Briefly glancing her way, he captured her hand giving it a gentle squeeze before turning his full attention back to the road. They still had a bit of distance to cover physically and emotionally.

"Josh, it seems to me that the gloom of the morning transforming into this beautiful Friday afternoon is a good omen. If our spur of the moment decision to come on this retreat needed validating, then this does it for me. The change in the weather and the fact two participants withdrawing left spaces for us to slot into. The synchronicity of right place and right timing works for me."

"Love how you think Cassie but can't deny my architect self was intrigued as soon as Michelle showed us the brochure. Old monastery, mud brick and timber construction were also drawcards for me. And we have two nights and three days to explore both the monastery and the Angels. For the moment let's enjoy the drive and the change of scene for both of us."

When Josh put on some soft tuneful classical music, Cassie settled back to relax and enjoy where this country road was taking them. Releasing any expectations about what may or may not happen when they reached their destination.

Cassie thought she may drift off, but then a review of the last six months began flowing through her mind. *The Angels must already be working* she thought briefly. Because she was viewing these events as though she was watching a movie, one in which she was an impartial observer and listener. Interestingly the movie opened by transporting her to the previous three months and especially to the past month.

Watching the movie unfold she was able to capture the moment when she finally acknowledged the growing tension between her and Josh. There still were many moments when grief carried them back to their usual closeness. This level of strain in their relationship was unusual and was rather difficult to admit to, because it wasn't just triggered by their grief, but made worse by their different ideas for moving forward. And for the first time in their marriage, they seemed unable to reach a compromise that suited them both.

Even watching the events unfold it seemed like years had passed as it now took her back to six months earlier when they had moved on from the initial shock of discovering that she was pregnant to becoming excited. Shock being their first emotions as her pregnancy was so unexpected and not on their well thought out timetable. Their future, planned for children, were scheduled for when she completed her Naturopathic training. She already had an established Herbalist practice, and looked forward to widening the scope of the services she could offer her existing and future clients. In those early days they could laugh when they took turns in quoting John Lennon's statement. "Life is what happens while you're busy making other plans."

Once they worked through their uncertainties, they were planning for, and joyfully anticipating the arrival of this new life they had created.

Nature unfortunately had another plan in store for them. After just passing the twelve-week mark when supposedly she had reached a considered safe stage, she miscarried. Their joyful anticipation ended abruptly being replaced by deep sadness, despair and the pain of having something precious ripped from them.

They were never in competition about whose grief was the greatest. They cried together shared their feelings, held and comforted one another. It was a roller coaster ride they were experiencing together.

For her included in the myriad of feelings was relief which was then followed by guilt. Intellectually she knew that she had accepted the gift of this pregnancy but also remembered feeling guilty about her initial feelings of shock and the thoughts about this not being the right time. She kept questioning had she been looking after herself, had she been eating the most nourishing foods, had she rested enough? Intellectually she knew she had.

The tension had grown because Josh's solution was for her to become pregnant again as soon as possible but she wished to wait and was starting to feel the strain of nudging him to remember that she only had one more semester to complete her degree.

She watched how Josh struggled to understand. The great strength in their relationship had always been their ability to communicate their feelings and resolve issues as they arose. She could picture her mental and emotional fingers crossed while trusting that strength was still there and hadn't been too weakened by grief.

While all these undercurrents were making their presence felt she saw herself caught up in a web of more what ifs. If she acquiesced to what Josh wanted, how would that feel? Would she become resentful? If she stood her ground and said what felt right for her at this time, would that damage their ongoing relationship?

All she could do was look ahead and hold fast to her trust, secure in the knowledge that yes, she wanted her relationship with Josh to thrive along with the future children they would be blessed with. But it was important to her to also build and trust her relationship with herself.

Going back and forward along her timeline the screen began to flicker with the final scenes bringing last night's dream and this morning into focus.

In the dream the soul that had been present in her womb began to converse with her 'I felt very welcome, but I could only be with you for a short time. My presence and my leaving were a gift to help you to get clear about what is true for you and to encourage you to awaken and follow the nudging of spirit to walk the path that will bring joy into your life. When I left, I wasn't lost, as a soul my life continues. I am light and love and will return in divine timing.'

On awakening she was filled with both sadness and joy. Sadness for their loss then joy and wonder that this little soul that had been in their lives so briefly would return. Tears flowed as she recounted the dream to Josh and wrote it in her journal.

Silence met the sharing of her dream. It wasn't an uncomfortable silence, but she sensed that they both needed time to digest her dreams' message and any possible discussion was put aside in the morning rush.

Precious Gems

Josh's "Earth to Cassie", brought her back to the present." Cassie, could you check the address and directions again. I am pretty sure I have taken the wrong turn!"

Noticing their surroundings, she laughed and agreed.

"Yes, Josh in the brochure I never saw a golf course mentioned. I think we are close. Let's check out the next right turn."

"This looks more like it and more as I expected. And look a sign. "Josh laughed.

As was their habit they would break into singing an appropriate song at moments like this and it always amazed them that they both came up with the same one. "Looks like we made it" seemed called for as they continued along the narrow winding dirt road bordered by impressive stands of gum trees and native shrubs.

Their singing fading out when they set out to follow the next set of directions of where to first unpack their car, before heading to repark in the designated area.

The afternoon was still sunny, the fresh country air was delightful to breathe and held no sense of rush. They were content to stop and take in their first view of the retreat centre's mud brick and timber construction. Its' appearance was both rustic and cosy. Being surrounded by sprawling gardens and walkways added to the charm.

They were just about to enter the object of their contemplation when their arrival was greeted by a woman with beautiful long flowing auburn hair. Her serene face and the light in her eyes immediately put them at ease.

"Welcome, as the only couple booked in you must be Cassie and Josh. My name is Crow and I have the pleasure of being your retreat facilitator this weekend. Come on in. After you get settled in your room and get your bearings, please make your way back to the dining room in about three quarters of an hour. We will all be ready for afternoon tea before the retreat officially gets underway.

Walking into their bedroom that was theirs for the weekend they were both delighted by the picture window that bought the outside inside and the glass door giving them instant access to explore the natural landscape beyond.

They used the time well, making the bed, with the sheets they were instructed to bring and hanging up the clothes that would benefit from being on hangers. With the remaining time left they set out to explore the twists and turns of the paved corridors while committing to memory the location of the bathrooms, meeting room and chapel before setting off to find the kitchen and dining room.

Meeting the other participants and the healthy afternoon tea had been such a treat and set a hopeful vibe for the outcome of the weekend. Cassie was enjoying the sensation that she was meeting up with friends, not strangers, simply ones they hadn't caught up with for a while. That sensation stayed with her and didn't fade during the introductory session. And spilled over into the welcome dinner which was filled with fun and laughter along with a delicious array of food to enjoy.

Josh, seated across the table from her was carrying on an animated conversation with an older woman whose name was Stella. Though she chastised herself for her thought, older, because Stella oozed a youthful vitality. Prior to meeting her officially she had noticed her across the room thinking what a delightful, colourful package she was. Smiling as she also noticed her naturally silver streaked brunette curls would flash and shimmer when her curls caught the light. Though petite, Cassie had the sensation that energetically Stella was quite tall. When she was being introduced to her she remembered feeling mesmerised by her twinkling blue eyes and the warmth they emanated seemed to envelope her in a hug.

As Friday evening unfolded into Saturday Cassie appreciated the wise words that Stella contributed to any of the sharing times. They always seemed to resonate with her, and Josh's quiet remarks revealed that he was having a similar experience.

Saturday then rolled into Sunday with another early start in the chapel before breakfast.

Before joining Josh and the others for breakfast Cassie made her way back to the chapel to collect her notebook that she inadvertently left there.

At the door of the Chapel, she stood transfixed by the sight of Stella on one of the timber pews. The light streaming through the stain glass windows seemed to penetrate her creating the effect that she was glowing. Stella looked transparent and yes, she was sitting, but her body was levitating and had risen at least ten centimetres off the seat. *This was a sight* she thought that she wasn't going to forget.

As though nothing unusual had happened Stella opened her eyes as her body slowly lowered and beckoned to her to sit next to her. "Cassie its lovely to get this one-to-one time with you. And I love seeing the changes that are visible on your face. It's reflecting the same lessening of the strain that's also leaving Josh's face. Are you sensing the presence of Angels? Crow is magical in her ability to call them into our presence."

"Thanks, Stella, for validating that I am feeling the subtle changes. Yes, while our intention is to resolve the strain that has made it into our relationship, would you believe Josh and I haven't had much time to talk about those tensions that brought us here. We have both been focused on what Crow is teaching us and yes revelling in the sensation of being surrounded by Angels. Our private conversations have been filled with discussing all we are hearing and learning.

I had a dream before coming on the weekend. We have put it on the back burner in our minds and know we will talk about it, but for now have been trying to stay present to what gems we are learning here."

For a moment they sat in a comfortable silence Stella breaking it to comment.

"Cassie you just used the word gems and that perfectly describes you and Josh. You are both precious gems in your own right. It's up to you individually to treasure and polish yourselves brightly so you can shine within first, then sharing and enjoying each other's sparkle."

Cassie loved that analogy and loved listening to Stella as she continued.

"Josh shared with me the cause of that tension along with the loss and sadness you have been living through. It's only natural for you both to feel stressed which in turn is creating tension especially as Josh's solution, which he also shared with me is 'let's make it happen now' and your wish to take a meandering path to get to the same place. It can seem hard when what feels right and true for you is opposite to what feels right for a loved one. All you can do is keep your loving communication open and share how you feel and trust that sensation you experience when you know what's true for you. That's what the gift of awareness or your inner observer will give you, it will wake you up to the thoughts going on in your mind. Awareness is not the thoughts but allows you to know that you do have the power of choice. You can then notice are your thoughts making up scenarios or putting conditions on all the aspects of your life and especially on love? Whether that be love for yourself or for another. The one thing you can always change are your thoughts. Sometimes in what seems the dark times of our lives we learn to treasure what is true about us and not made up."

"Thanks Stella I think this weekend is bringing us back to appreciating ourselves and how we are with each other. Being precious gems is a beautiful image to hold onto and will continue to refer to, along with the image of a meandering path."

Sitting in a comfortable silence Cassie could picture in her mind her and Josh as gems and the meandering path that she felt strongly was the one for her to take. But she knew she needed to dig deep and find the courage within her to take and stay on that path and ask Josh for six months to wait for her to catch up so that both their needs could come to fruition in the fullness of time. She thought again of what she'd decided before coming on this weekend, that she didn't wish to agree with Josh just for the sake of peace and then feel resentful for giving in.

"Stella all I am asking for is six months. Then I know I will be ready for the next desired chapter in our lives."

She was experiencing a feeling of deep satisfaction in being able to be so open about expressing her needs without any fears of being judged or questioned about her priorities.

Continuing to sit quietly together, it seemed to Cassie that they were both being bathed by the warming light streaming through the chapel windows.

Stella took her hand and squeezed it before saying.

"It's been three months since your miscarriage and add to that the six months you are negotiating for, that equals nine months, an appropriate gestation period for you to evolve into an even more loving, joyful and courageous woman. One who knows the difference between the feelings generated from made up scenarios and the feelings based in truth, ones you can trust. I so look forward to watching you unfurl.

Cassie, neither you nor Josh have done anything wrong, life is about facing the difficulties with honesty. Exploring the obstacles, releasing whatever is necessary and rebuilding or rather tuning back into your natural love and joy especially if they seem as though they are missing. But in fact, love and joy don't go missing, for a while we can simply stop seeing them. I encourage you to look at your life to see whether it supports you by allowing joy to be part of all you do, or does it prevent joy? That's for you alone to discern. And something each of us needs to do.

Cassie these words are just flooding through my mind and may prove helpful. I think they are for you and for me as they are in first person.

'Life is a noun. To live is a verb. Living my life is a sentence. What sort of life am I sentencing myself to? One that creates joy or drains it?' "

Cassie let those words sink and repeated them silently to herself as she thought of how to apply them to all the areas of her life before asking.

"It's not as simple as trusting my own feelings, is it? It's discerning what feelings I make up and react to and what are real and true for me. That would help create joy, wouldn't it?"

Again, Stella squeezed her hand, "Yes, and you are a discerning young woman and hopefully still young enough to enjoy some words by Dr Seuss.'

Somewhat surprised she nodded her head wondering what Stella had in mind.

'Today you are you! That is truer than true! There is no one alive who is you-er than you!'

A big smile spread across Cassie's face and in turn squeezing Stella's hand she could no longer hold back from asking.

"Stella before coming on this workshop Josh and I were used to being on the same page and I have been worrying that maybe we aren't even in the same chapter let alone book. But I am wondering Stella why did you come to this weekend, you seem to have such an abundance of knowledge, wisdom and are so joyful?"

"Ahhh Cassie you are sweet and that's a nice way of asking 'why?' When I am so many years older than you and Josh and all the other participants. My age is exactly the reason I am here. Yes, I have walked the path ahead of you, but I now find myself at another one of life's crossroads unsure about which way to go. I have never liked the word retirement. It's a word that feeds my uncertainties and highlights my reluctance to make any changes. I am still working but can't quite grasp for how much longer or what new paths await. My senses tell me I need to make some changes and be ready and open for what's next for me. One of my clients suggested to me that I would know when that time comes.

 Barry and I never had children together and our children with our previous spouses are grown adults. The grandchildren are also headed towards adulthood and living busy lives.

We have been self-employed for most of our working lives and just recently Barry has wound up his business and is ready to roam. I have been a therapist for well over thirty years and part of my uncertainty is that I am not sure what my future would be like without seeing clients. I have been trialling cutting back on my availability and must admit my physical body enjoys the lightening of the load. I love the interaction and can't help but wonder who I will be without that?"

With a smile on her face Stella added.

"Cassie we are somewhat in the same boat. My decision needs to be based on what's right for me not on what might suit others. Barry as always doesn't step in and try to influence my choices. It's all me who is carrying the heavy load of obligation and fear of letting people down."

If she hadn't been so intent on watching the expressions that were crossing Stella's face, she might have missed that even for Stella the last words she'd uttered were a revelation, a light bulb moment.

With an even bigger smile on her face Stella continued quietly.

"Cassie I am so grateful that in talking to you I can now pinpoint what exactly is the fear that's been keeping me stuck and this may sound weird to you, but I felt a hand between my shoulder blade pushing me on my way to this weekend. It's a sensation I have had many times throughout my life, and I always trust it to send me in the direction that's best for me."

Nodding her head as Stella spoke Cassie understood that she and generations even younger than hers didn't have a monopoly on the need to discern the best possible paths on which to flourish and live life to the full.

Rising to finally make their way to breakfast Stella smiled again while bringing Cassie's attention back to her earlier words.

"Cassie there are lots of pages in a chapter and there are lots of pages in a book. You have a lot of scope to work from and rewrite the ending of this chapter in your lives and start a new one. Take heart if you weren't at least in the same book neither of you would be here."

As the morning rolled on Cassie was aware that any remaining tension had been replaced with a sense of deep peace. Each time she and Josh looked at one another their smiles were back in their eyes.

Crow had just discussed what was on the program for this afternoon then announced some free time to spend how they wished before their final group lunch.

On their way to find a nice place to sit in the garden they waved to Stella who was setting off on a walk. Cassie couldn't help but notice the whiteness of her joggers. They must be new she thought.

"Cassie, 'Josh called her attention away from watching Stella disappear along the path." Can we talk about your dream? I also need to tell you that I had a similar one and if I have learnt nothing else this weekend it is to trust the power of synchronicity. And I also believe that you and I have the same desire to create a family together. I apologise about how rigid and unrealistic I have been in wanting it to happen right away. Maybe that was my way of coping with grief, and I haven't been fair in not listening to you."

Tears streamed down Josh's face as he came to the end of his words and Cassie simply reached out to hug him at the same time as he placed his arms around her. With their arms wrapped around each other they both leaned back asking "did you feel that?"

"Yes, "Cassie whispered, "that may be what they mean by being touched by an Angel, a healing one at that.'

Wiping his tears from his cheeks Josh also whispered, "I am definitely not disbelieving as that is what it felt like to me too."

"Josh I am so happy we came on this weekend. Whatever life has in store for us we can get through it together and by remembering to ask the Angels for help, we will not only survive but will thrive."

It was pure joy to sit and just be together, separating only when they heard the lunch bell.

By the time they made it to the dining room Cassie noticed everyone gathered all except that one presence that both her and

Josh found so comforting to be in. She had been delighted by Josh's news that Stella lived close to their own home and wished to stay in contact with them.

Concerned by her absence Cassie asked Crow if Stella had returned from her walk.

Crow looked at her and without any apparent concern accompanied by a mysterious smile commented.

"Cassie enjoy your lunch, don't worry about Stella. She will be back she's flying about somewhere."

Although she wondered about the meaning of that mysterious smile Cassie rejoined Josh and settled into enjoying another delicious meal and stimulating conversation.

 # STELLA 

The Cage

The dampness seeping through her shoes was starting to make its presence felt and had her looking down to find that she was standing in a puddle. Not a deep one but still held enough water to creep through the soles of her shoes and transfer the dampness to her socks and her feet. Stella looked around feeling rather lost and panicky for a moment unable to work out where she was and what she was doing hemmed in by trees and thick bushes on this wet narrow track. Added to the panic was a sense of confusion as she couldn't understand what had happened. Had she lost her memory or was she experiencing one of those brain fugue states she recently had been reading about. This was followed by the momentary thought but that was in a *fiction book.*

Of course, the practical thing to do was to step out of the puddle, but that didn't change the fact that the path was damp and strewn with large clumps of soggy vegetation. Noticing that her breaths were short and shallow she started taking some deep breaths and was happy to sense that her heart which had been racing was beginning to slow down. *Wouldn't be good to have a blood pressure spike* here she thought, wherever here was.

Her brain began to kick into gear as she started to remember that it'd seemed like a good idea to use the weekend's retreat free time for a walk. The track she recalled was an easy one wide and well maintained. The trees created a beautiful canopy against a deep blue sky. They weren't too dense to prevent the bright sunshine from providing a dappled light along the pathway before her. What had happened? How had she ended up in this damp gloomy place?

Voices admonishing her for leaving the walking track filled her head. Her long-passed mother's voice was in amongst all the chatter 'now just look at those new walking shoes. And why did you choose white? Will take you a bit to get those clean.' For a moment she remembered as a much younger person whenever she was leaving the family home, she had needed to pass her mother's inspection about how she had looked. Knowing now that what her mother was really worried about was how she appeared to the outside world. What would people think if everything wasn't just so?

Thanks mum she thought as if she wasn't feeling stupid enough and found it hard to refrain from telling herself so. Then lots of voices were having a go. Some trying to be friendly others a bit strident in their opinions of her predicament. She felt immobilised and unable to get clear about what to do next. Then the gentlest 'shhh' started to resound through her head and on hearing this the voices gradually began to quieten. It was as if they all sensed someone else was in charge. And as the volume lessened and began to abate, she heard another 'shhh' followed by a gentle voice urging her stop listening to all that noise and instead listen to the birds. As she tuned in, Stella noticed that they were singing a beautiful melody, one she'd never heard before. After giving her some space to listen, the gentle voice continued.

"Now turn your attention to the sound of the water as it was that sound that brought you here."

The practical side of Stella came to the fore again remembering that she was inland, not on the coast, there were no rivers or creeks on this property, none chartered anyway. The only body of water she remembered seeing was the lotus flower pond near the retreat centre.

Those thoughts earned her another firm but gentle and longer 'shhhhhh.'

"Come on Stella you were so happy and at peace to leave the path. You were flying and enjoying the freedom as you rose up and floated through the treetops. It would seem as though some old lingering fears and doubts triggered your innate ability to embrace this sense of limitless freedom. Take some more deep breaths. Please trust me when I say no harm will come to you. Come follow the sound. I have been waiting for you."

Had she been happy to leave the path she wondered as she continued to look around? That idea seemed impossible when she observed the seemingly impregnable dark hedge in front of her. Her feet were not only wet they were starting to feel cold and where was the dappled sunshine? But it was beginning to sink in that the shoosh voice had been right, she could hear water. Not a rush or a possibly damaging roar but water tinkling along and similar to the song of the birds rather melodious.

The gentle voice was starting to woo her again.

"Sometimes Stella when you and many others sense and taste the freedom to be the magnificent limitless beings you really are, just a slight taste of that can cause doubts and fears to resurface and recreate old familiar patterns. Do you remember the poem you wrote so many years ago about being in a cage? Lines from that poem include.

'Life's become a pattern of looking through the bars.

Of allowing doubt and fear to outweigh love, joy, laughter and awe.'

Stella, you found the power to bend those bars and step out. Look around, all that's happening here is that you have recreated that cage. Perhaps you have set a little test for yourself, or you are anxious about what life would be like to finally be free of those worn-out fears and doubts."

Looking around, she had no other explanation except to accept that her mind must have created her present circumstances and noted that it did indeed have a prison like feel. As she focused on the dense hedge in front of her, at first, she thought her eyes were getting weary and playing tricks on her as a bright, shimmering light swirled at her eye level and grew into the shape of a slender hand.

"Stella when you are ready take my hand and step through the hedge you will find that it isn't solid at all. During your sleep states you have taken my hand and stepped into the world beyond this hedge many times. This is the first time you have been wide awake. Such joy awaits you because this time when you return to your everyday life you will remember being here. The seeds you have planted here are flourishing and eager for you to re discover their ongoing role of nourishing you.

Can you remember what you said to the young woman who is also attending the retreat? She was sharing some of her concerns with you perhaps saying your own words out loud may inspire and help you too."

Stella remembered talking to Cassie, she was anxious about what others would think about the possible changes she wished to make in her life.

"Ok, this is what I said. Life is a noun. To live is a verb. Living my life is a sentence. What sort of life am I sentencing myself to?"

Listening to her own words Stella looked around and understood that she could sentence herself to a life back in a cage or move forward through that hedge.

The now fully visible hand beckoned to her and gradually Stella felt brave enough to reach out and take it. As she did so she was immediately filled with an incredible sensation of peace, and at the same time marveled at how quickly trust had replaced her initial distrust. A knowing buried deep within her instinctively knew that peace was always present and was bewildered about having needed to re-experience her past wounds and the limits she had put on herself. Then recalling the poem, the gentle voice had reminded her that in that poem, light, love and joy were also with her in the cage. Perhaps sometimes hidden but nonetheless always with her. Another gentle squeeze of her hand heightened her awareness to the return of these familiar energies flowing through her. The flow rapidly becoming a delightful surge.

Stella felt the need to close her eyes as the hand attached to the gentle voice tenderly pulled her forward. The momentum of this movement dissolved what previously had seemed an impregnable barrier. Opening her eyes to slits she glanced back and could only see the safe and dappled sunshine path of her walk.

Moving her head forward again while maintaining contact with the powerful warm hand she opened her eyes fully and was amazed to behold colourful atoms and molecules arranging themselves to take on the form of a stunning female.

Her gaze roamed over the magnificence of the soft flowing fabric draped around this Being, who both puzzled her and at the same time felt familiar. Her attention was captured by the sight of her robe like dress rather than focusing on the questions that were forming in her mind. The dress was of the softest blue yet in the folds she could see a darker deeper blue with touches of flashing silver. When this beautiful Being moved to stand in front of her the movement created a shimmering wave effect like ripples across a pond. Like a magnet Stella's gaze was drawn to the most beautiful eyes she had ever seen, which again had a sense of familiarity.

Those eyes which were twinkling with both welcome and delight were framed in an alluring soft rounded face surrounded by fine, curly, shining dark tresses. With a big smile on her face, she bowed her head towards Stella and that gentle shoosh voice she had heard earlier began speaking softly.

"Welcome home to the Fairy and Elemental kingdom Stella, I am Yakazan. This may seem confusing for a little while, but I am an aspect of you as you are of me. You chose to take human form and I remained here as your welcoming committee for whenever you returned during your sleep or meditation states. I am one of the higher vibrations of you on the inner planes. We have maintained a connection that when you are here also extends to being telepathic. You chose the veil of forgetfulness before setting out on your earth walk. Accepting that it wouldn't be what you knew here. You fully intended on your incarnation to experience the many expressions of life in human form and walk the path known as spiritual evolution.

Some time has passed since you set that initial intention and you are now ready to reset it to remembering. It's not coincidental Stella what's happening for you as the veils between our world and Mother Earth are lifting and becoming transparent. Earth is moving through her own evolution to higher vibrations similar to the energy and vibration of our realm which is also rapidly increasing and moving us to higher dimensions. I've heard you often say Stella as well as your thoughts about strapping in for what feels like a roller coaster ride. You may as well enjoy it."

"Yakazan I probably don't need to think or say this, but this is way different to what I experience day to day. I am used to the spoken word and even as I learn to appreciate this telepathic link, I will probably fall back into what's familiar. But I can also quieten my thoughts and listen."

After sharing those few words, Stella not only saw but experienced the energy of the smile that passed across Yakazan's face and happily settled into being both fascinated and attentive as more of Yakazan's words began flowing into her mind.

"Be mindful Stella that words whether spoken or ones that arrive as thoughts carry the good intentions of the sender to the receiver. That holds true for all forms of communication. That's a whole topic that we could discuss at length and before we move off it, I ask you to simply notice the energy behind your words. Loving words aren't received as such if spoken angrily. And if you are angry, it calls for clear honest, non-blaming conversation. Or if you are only saying nice things to someone so they will do something nice for you. But rather than discern more examples let's move back to settling your confusion about where you are."

"I do endeavour to be thoughtful about how I deliver my words though I may not always be successful. But back to now, I have just broken through a hedge to get off a track and would like to get back on track with what you said earlier 'this is not a dream.'

Will I really remember it?"

That earned her another one of those powerfully charged smiles.

"You will remember, and I am here to remind you Stella that you chose to incarnate on Mother Earth and before you left here, you planted seeds so you could develop and use them on your earth walk. Just like the heart in your human body activates to pump blood throughout your body and your human brain activates and send signals to fire your nerves. The seeds you planted here activated whenever you required them to help guide you through many of the circumstances, situations and challenges that appear to be part of the human condition. I know that one of the purposes you assigned to yourself was to help humans learn how to play more and enjoy who they are and what they have, as well as drawing their attention to cease thinking that there is something wrong with them."

Stella was astonished to hear the origins of her sense that there was something wrong with her. Which was often accompanied by her internal question about where did she fit? She had struggled with both for many years and found comfort in the fact that it had served a purpose, not just for herself, but was one that had led her on a path to guide others.

Yakazan's words were colliding and replaying in her head. Experience, purpose, overcoming, healing and guiding others to also let go of the belief that there is something wrong with them. The astonishment to finally know where this sense of wrongness had originated was staying with her and she let it find space within her as she tuned back into what else Yakazan was saying.

"The seeds I mentioned are what the human part of you would call buried treasure but buried is a relative term as you never buried them so deep that you can't find them. The term 'in place' may be better as you planted them in place for your continued use. It's your human form that most needs the seeds you created for your completion and fulfillment on the Earthly plane. Here you always are a treasured treasure."

Remembering Home

Still feeling amazed by what Yakazan had already told her Stella couldn't help but wonder again if all this was just her imagination? Questioning was she really awake and was this real? For a moment Stella forgot her telepathic connection with Yakazan but was quickly reminded by Yakazan breaking into her thoughts with.

"Oh, precious one it is never just your imagination."

The sounds of chuckles drew her attention back to Yakazan's smiling face.

"Yes Stella, I assure you once again, you are awake, and this is real. I know it's a lot to take in as humans do tend to overthink things and think there's no place like Mother Earth.

On this visit as you look around you are only seeing this layer. Throughout the universe there are layers within layers and that's the same for all living things. Rather like that Black Forest Cake you like. Every layer needs the other layers to support the other."

Stella's shaky confidence was boosted by Yakazan's assurance again that this was real and as she slowly looked around, it was not only her eyes that seemed to open wider, but all her senses seemed to switch on. The scent of the air could only be described as pure with a sweet and fresh taste and touched her skin like a soft caress, and she could hear the whispers of delight floating around her and beyond.

The only words that came to her that was even close to describing the movement of the air around her was that it was filled with ions of joy.

Stella couldn't help but feel transfixed by the clarity and beauty of the vista spread out around her. Looking ahead she could see a waterfall which was so clear she thought it was liquid light. Again, hearing that thought Yakazan explained.

"The water in this waterfall is life giving and stepping under it is both restorative and rejuvenating as well as being cleansing. You will see scattered around the main pool smaller pools but not small in the power of their vibrations and healing powers. You may also notice the colour differences which indicates the healing properties of each pool. Many, like yourself, arrive here in a sleep state or just prior to sleep then decide which pool to immerse yourselves in. Stella, you have often chosen the energy charge of the golden pool enjoying the surge of the golden bubbles permeating all your cells. Sometimes you have chosen pink when you wish to fill yourself with the higher vibrations of radiant love energy and of course violet when you need to release the cause and effects of hurts and emotional wounds."

Maintaining her gaze in that direction Stella was also able to discern periodic plumes of colourful misty sprays arising from each pool. She experienced a surge of delight before moving her gaze to take in the green fields and the profusion of multi coloured flowers which seemed to spontaneously spring up everywhere and bordered the pathways that led her eyes to take in the trees in the distance. She was able to extend her vision to patches of green beyond where she could see flashes of reflected light from more bodies of water surrounded by stone and crystal dwellings some tiny, and some large with various sizes in between.

Her gaze then coming to rest on orbs of light that were in constant motion in the trees. Fairy lights she thought but unlike her tree lights at home these didn't need to be plugged in.

While taking all this in Stella kept noticing out of the corner of her eye a shimmering movement by the waterfall. And watched in wonder as the shimmer transformed into the shape of a beautiful woman for a moment, then back into a glistening light body. While in her woman form, she cupped her hands into the main pool then poured the water over her body.

Yakazan's soothing voice broke into her sense of wonder.

"Stella, you will get to meet the liquid light woman that your eyes keep retuning to soon, I know she wishes to speak to you. But right now, your energy is beginning to adjust to being here. I know it's a lot to take in. You are in another dimension in your human form and yet you can see grass, trees, waterfalls. Although time is perceived differently here there are still the changes of light in what you call night and day. As you adjust you will be able to make out more shapes in what you presently perceive as movement and air currents around you. You may have forgotten that fairies can be shy but like revelers at a party they are surrounding you."

Tremendous feelings of longing to stay in this place began to fill Stella which resulted in Yakazan's still calm voice breaking into those yearning sensations in a slightly firmer tone.

"No, Stella if you were able to truly see everything on this visit and reignite your deep bond with this dimension you would never want to leave. Now isn't the time for you to stay as you do need to return to Mother Earth. You have your mission to complete along with many other light workers who continue to be a part of Earth's healing. The movies you see on big and small screens and the copious number of stories written about scary aliens that wish to wreak havoc on planet earth as well as inflict pain and confusion upon humans are neither true nor ever likely to be true. With certain truthfulness I can say that Light workers from across the known and unknown Universe, Galaxies and beyond are connected by a united purpose to contribute, guide and be a part of Earth's healing. This oneness of connection is their normal state of being and their desire is to deliver this awareness to all who inhabit Mother Earth."

While still taking in her surroundings Stella couldn't help but wonder about the value of her own contribution to supporting the healing of Mother Earth and her fellow humans.

"Ahhhhh Stella, I hear your thoughts again. Your contribution is by no means small. I realise that in your mind you have held the thought that you have never needed to know. You call it 'not investing in outcomes' but you have touched the lives of others through your one-to-one work and with groups. Even when you go shopping you spread your smile around. Everything you do has had a ripple effect especially to those who you have reminded that the Power of their life choices lies in their own hands. Then you follow this with encouraging them to stand in their own truth and to be the very best versions of themselves that they can. Your connection with them is joyful and in turn they have a sense of connection or oneness with you that propels them into experiencing that with those who are a part of their own life journey's. In this way the awareness of oneness and joy flows on like a river, connecting and re connecting as many on earth as possible. So yes Stella, you will return to your everyday life but as I said on your arrival this time you will remember this whole experience. You will continue to inspire and gift others with your healing presence. Now come on Stella, first things first we have a stop to make before the discoveries and purpose of your visit is revealed."

Stella could feel some old doubts surfacing but then as she looked around again there were no doubts that this was all happening and that she was awake. She thought for a moment that perhaps it was time to trust that this was real. She was here and there was no way her imagination, powerful as it sometimes was, could dream this up. So yes, maybe she could finally accept that she really did have a healing presence and that perhaps she didn't need to put so much effort into being what she already was.

First Things First

Stella began to notice that her practical and relaxed retreat clothes were transforming into something that felt both soft and silky. An unusual garment presenting a paradox for her as it felt loose and yet at the same time snug, which created a sense of cozy warmth against her skin. As she glanced down her body she also appeared to be glowing. Just as she was taking this in Yakazan beckoned Stella to follow, giving her a view, for the first time, of the silvery wings among the folds of her gown.

Moving ahead of her Yakazan seemed to glide rather than walk and of course her human brain latched onto the image of a hoverboard. She remembered seeing one years ago in the "Back to The Future" movies. While some way-out science fiction ideas had become part of Earth's everyday reality, hover boards weren't one of them. She couldn't help but smile when the thought *that the ability to make such an item hadn't really gotten off the ground,* popped into her mind. Instead of allowing her mind to distract her by searching for examples of what way-out ideas did become real. She reined in this line of thinking to bring her focus back to Yakazan 's silvery wings and to taking great care of where she placed her feet. Even if she couldn't fully see everything, she became aware of movement and changes in the vibrations around her. Seemingly out of nowhere a thought flashed through her mind that Pixies, while good natured were often prone to play tricks and her human ears were becoming attuned to delighted whispers that tinkled like soft musical notes being carried through the air.

"Seems like some veils of forgetting are lifting." Was accompanied by one of Yakazan's delightful chuckles.

"The Sylphs would love to catch up with you, but I don't think it is going to be possible. They ask that you keep working with them in all weather-related matters. The Sylphs love that you call on them often. Though they can't always fulfill your desire to keep the skies above your clothesline dry and asked me to pass on that sometimes it just needs to rain."

Smiling at Yakazan's words, Stella recalled the times when she was traveling or driving and despite the weather forecast, they had really helped her out by creating perfect days for her to experience and be safe. Putting aside her curiosity of Yakazan's words, 'first things first' Stella began noticing sensations and feelings of homecoming flowing through her and as natural as breathing, they began attaching to and intensifying the feelings of intense longing she had experienced earlier. But having time to explore these feelings also needed to be put aside as she trailed behind yet at the same time easily kept up with Yakazan.

They were moving further into an area of dense trees that seemed to welcome and embrace her. The trees formed a natural canopy while the fairies and their orbs added light and vibrant energy to the forest they were moving through. Areas that would have otherwise been dark were illuminated. Nervousness and excitement were battling for prominence within her when she was startled by the ease with which she was beginning to accept her telepathic link with Yakazan. Excitement came to the fore and was accompanied by what could only be described as a crescendo of joy rising within as her mind connected with Yakazan's and this joy was further heightened by the knowledge that it was flowing through them both. Her intense focus on this joy was halted yet in no way diminished when Yakazan unexpectedly stopped. With a flutter of her wings and a sweep of her light filled hands Yakazan drew Stella's attention to a pulsating pyramid nestled in a circle of tall trees.

"In a moment Stella, we will enter your personal sacred crystal light pyramid. You have been here often during some of your meditation sessions as well as numerous times in your sleep state. You are only too aware of the effects that negative energy and thoughts patterns can have on your physical body. Humans seem to have ways of attracting negativity from many sources. Some land on you from those around you. Wherever it comes from negativity can so easily slip in and accumulate not only in your body but also affects both your mind and spirit. Stella this isn't new information, you have also experienced these effects in situations that you could normally handle with ease, but instead, quickly spiraled into states of overwhelm and anxiety. At such times you found yourself being reactive rather than creative. Fortunately, when you realised where your thoughts were taking you and the changes, they wrought in your energy field, you instinctively returned to this sacred healing space to cleanse the toxic effects of negativity. These sessions restored you to your natural balance and higher vibrations."

The truth of Yakazan's words brought tears to her eyes. She felt validated that each encounter here had been real, not fantasy. Even though her tears began to flow down her cheeks she was experiencing a euphoric sensation of joy, delight, wonder and love all wrapped up together which served to increase her sense of homecoming. Stepping further inside she was delighted to see that what she had previously thought was the product of her visualising ability, was there in place simply waiting for her presence. Her gaze took in the crystal table, and she knew from each journey that she'd taken on it that it was like lying on liquid and not hard as one would expect crystal to be.

The table was flanked by two crystal chairs and a shimmering stalactite suspended above the table from the pyramid's apex reflected light onto the surrounding walls. Her memories were providing her mind with the information that during previous healing sessions the colours could change and increase to whatever vibration she needed at that time. And there below the table was the gentle yet powerful violet flame that absorbed whatever she released into it and looked with gratitude again to the brilliant light emanating from the stalactite as she remembered the role it played in re-energising all her cells.

The words 'let's sit for a moment', were spoken gently by Yakazan and as they both sat the crystal chairs began to glow even brighter.

"Stella, this may come across as a lesson to you and perhaps some components of what I share with you are. But in a few moments, it will also be a trip down memory lane for you. As I mentioned earlier you passed through the veil of forgetfulness when you incarnated on earth, so of course you had spiritual amnesia about your purpose and your connection to the non-physical world. That veil may have obscured your view, but it didn't create any separation between us. I was always with you, and I have always been with you. I was there when you, as a young child, you wandered for hours on end lost in the beauty which surrounded you. Your faithful border collie protected you as did I. Though your ramblings weren't viewed as safe or appreciated by your birth mother."

Smiling at that memory Stella remembered that her wanderings as a three-year-old drove her mother to being desperate enough to tie a rope around her waist leaving enough length for her to run around before tying the other end around the tree in her back yard.

"I was also with you as you grew and could walk safely, with your mother's approval, through nature. You enjoyed bush walks, especially ones where you delightedly discovered hidden pools of water and fast flowing creeks. I was with you when diving into the ocean waves was sheer pleasure for you. That pleasure dimmed when fear took its place after that frightening and exhausting experience of being pounded and tumbled in a powerful surf's undertow. Since that day you now look for gentle waves and bay like conditions. Then I was there with you lying on the grass on a summer's night smothered in the scent of citronella leaves gazing with longing at a star filled night sky. And certainly, there when your singing and dancing would lift the spirits of your earth family whenever gloom settled upon them. And definitely with you during all the magical moments you have experienced throughout your earth life."

During Yakazan's retelling of some of these early memories Stella's crystal chair began to emit a slight vibration. She was astonished and felt comforted at the same time to know that she had never been alone in those moments. But rather than distract herself with searching for more standout memories she brought her attention back to Yakazan sensing she had more to say.

Smiling Yakazan continued, "Stella you chose human form but many beings from our lineage chose to retain their fairy form when they transitioned to Mother Earth. Like you they also have a purpose which includes supporting Earth, and one way they do this is to seek regions of dense and negative energy. They toil in these locations to absorb this negativity without any damage to their light bodies. Their service results in raising the vibrations that humans who pass in and out of these areas experience as an increase in joyfulness and playfulness in their hearts. Nature in these locations also takes on a healthier appearance as trees, plants and flowers thrive. They rejoice when humans are said to be 'off with fairies' but unfortunately, they know only too well that this simple statement is sometimes meant as an insult and not respected as something delightful to experience. Likewise, your own fairy DNA will quiver around beings of high vibration. That is why you Stella, are mindful about the vibrations you move in and out of. Around those of similar vibration and those who wish to awaken their energies, you open like a flower does to the sun's light.

To answer your heard but unasked question 'why are you here?'

It's time to stop forgetting!"

Yakazan's explanation and her already heightened senses triggered more memories to rise easily to the surface. Despite it having been spoken of earlier, there they were again. Thoughts, that had become a reoccurring theme running through her life 'was this real or was this imagined? 'Followed by 'did she really wish to remember?' As these thoughts played out in her mind, the feeling of being confused was making its presence felt. Generally, she was enthusiastic and willing to joyfully jump in when presented with healing opportunities or spending time exploring her inner world. Yet here she was experiencing tremors of resistance.

Finally, a flash of clarity brought with it the memory that it's ok to be confused and that it's often present in the beginning stages when undertaking any type of transformation. A state she had spoken about many times with others. *She'd stepped out of the cage* she admonished herself, this was real the crystal table was real not a figment of her imagination.

As they often turned up having a similar energetic impact it was hard to discern whether she was now feeling nervous or excited. She was experiencing both she realised and was grateful they replaced her earlier resistance and the resulting confusion. Clarity was always a welcome sensation as was her radical acceptance, that yes, it was time to once again lie on the crystal bed which had featured in so many of her visualisations and dreams.

As she gracefully settled on the table, familiar delicious and lasting sensations of previous healings flowed through. The effects of each process had certainly been real, not imagined, and had helped her to continue growing spiritually on her earth walk. Along with these familiar sensations she began to notice the stirrings of her usual enthusiasm. She was being offered a momentous gift. The ability to activate within her the power to remember.

Stella then heard the humour in Yakazan's voice once again assuring her.

"Stella think, of what's involved in cleaning a fish tank. You not only replace the water with fresh, but you also clear out the sludge that settles on the bottom of the tank. This is your time to clear out the sludge."

Once comfortable her body fused with ease, to the table's pulsating energy that seamlessly aligned with the gentle melodious sounds that had begun resonating throughout the chamber. Stella, with eyes closed sensed rather than saw Yakazan move to the head of the table and the Violet Flame below the table igniting. From previous experience she knew there was such a power in the Violet Flame that everything it absorbs is completely dissolved, forgiven, transformed, transmuted and healed.

As Stella relaxed further, she sensed a new determination arising within her to release any remaining blockages that would prevent her from recovering her memories and to cease forgetting. Therefore, she was amazed when guilt surfaced into her awareness. Guilt that she had ever left her home on the Inner Planes, for having separated from the Creator and this realm of love, joy and light. This unnecessary load of guilt was quickly followed by the realisation that any thought of separation had only been in her mind. Acknowledging this acted like pulling the plug on known and unknown blockages that were taking up space within her and obstructing her memories of home.

The experience of the sludge layer of her wanting and self judgements began to gurgle through this opening. The wanting to be perfect, to not make mistakes, to be liked and loved. The desire to apply that to herself, wanting to be thoughtful at all times. The wanting to release all her unfounded fears and doubts that were still trapped in that mire. Sitting alongside these doubt and fears were the lies she had told herself about what she could or couldn't do and achieve. The mistakes she had made in her communication that she had failed to correct in the moment. Words misspoken which then became unintentional lies fearing that to correct what was uttered would then make her appear foolish. But then that had only happened once she justified to herself, then in the next instance every justification she had ever believed she had ever needed to make to justify her very existence in life tumbled through her into the Violet Flame.

The vibration and energy of the stalactite in the apex of the pyramid rapidly increased. To Stella it felt like a laser beam of light searing right through her mental, emotional and physical body seeking out anything else that may still be hidden and any more roadblocks that her human self had put in the way of being and living as a miracle of light and love. Amazingly what arose into her awareness were the dark tentacles of anxiety. Childhood anxieties of not fitting in. The loss of confidence in her teenage years, the anxiety of trying to meet others' expectations as an adult and the present anxiety of not having enough energy or time to keep up with all she still wished to be and do. Of how she looked. Was she dressed appropriately? The anxiety of meeting new people. What would they think of her? Then the anxiousness of travel and getting from one place to another on time. If anyone had ever asked her, she would have denied that she was an anxious person. Yet here it was a tsunami of revealed and disturbed emotions pouring out of every cell in which any anxiety along with the cause and effects had been long held. The word anxious had gone so long without being acknowledged that the waves created by this tsunami were extremely uncomfortable and bordered on being painful as they surged through her.

This purging continued until the wave delivered her to what felt like calm shores, and as they receded, she began to experience light and joy flooding all her cells physically and emotionally. The stalactite activated once more to diffuse an even brighter light through Stella. And in that moment, she felt a rise in her physical body's ability to absorb and retain more light. Again, knowing without seeing it Stella sensed the Violet Flame dimming and taking with it all that it had dissolved. The laser light beam settled to a warm and inviting glow and the sound frequencies of the pyramid's crystal walls settled to a melodious discreet hum bringing this powerful and penetrating healing process to completion. Many sensations were flooding her. She was immensely grateful and beyond content that she'd overcome her initial resistance to begin this process of remembering.

Yakazan only needed to place a gentle hand on Stella's shoulder for her to arise without effort and return to her crystal chair.

With eyes closed Stella focused on her breathing. Each breath as it moved through her body was fresh and clear and seemed to arise like bubbles to the surface from a deep place within her that glowed pure and innocent. These shining bubbles of delight and wonder that filled her, accompanied the knowing that this innocence buried deep within her held no wrongness or guilt. Innocence so substantial that it couldn't be damaged by anything she had done or had been inflicted by another was a concept she welcomed with an overwhelming sense of relief. She reminded herself that this wasn't a dream that she was experiencing. This moment was real. Her innocence was her, perfect in its brilliance and she was determined she would never allow such brilliance to be dimmed again. Perhaps this was the buried treasure Yakazan had spoken of which had been obscured by her own thoughts, doubts and the concerns of playing the life of a human in a world that had sought to change her innocence.

Wrapped in the pure, joyful childlike vibrations, Stella moved her focus to the other sensations that were flowing through her. She could feel the residue effects of this powerful healing experience seeping into every cell and aspect of her being, mental, emotional and physical. Stella reveled in these sensations and in one of those light bulb moments she realised that the word 'embodiment' finally had a tangible meaning for her. It surpassed knowing something to be true to the reality of all her physical senses experiencing such deeply felt sensations. The fires of self-love were fanned from a spark into the brightest, colourful flames which also rose to the surface of her awareness. There was so much rising from the depths of her to light her way especially on pathways that she had forgotten.

Stella felt as though she was suspended in a state of pure bliss, a space that was so inviting to remain in. Yakazan's statement 'first things first' made perfect sense to her now. Releasing the sludge layer during this healing experience propelled her into a more fully awakened state.

To consciously remain conscious had always been part of her spiritual quest on earth.

Gratitude and the energy of a smile filled her as she thought of Yakazan's role in helping her span the bridge from forgetting to remembering. Her smile becoming even wider as she remained aware that Yakazan heard her thoughts, the difference now being she could also hear some of Yakazan's thoughts more clearly. Thoughts that were now penetrating her state of bliss encouraging her to open her eyes, enticing her with the idea that more discoveries awaited her and reminded her that it was also the process of rediscovering what had always been true about her which would also help her to lead others to the Truth of who they are.

Opening her eyes Stella noticed how fresh and vibrant she felt and that Yakazan appeared wrapped in that same childlike vibration. One that was also reflecting the brightest of smiles and an even more radiant presence. And in that moment, she was transfixed by the love emanating from Yakazan's eyes before hearing her softly spoken words.

"Stella I am only reflecting you and your restored natural innocence that you had concealed from your view."

Taking a moment to absorb Yakazan's words Stella then knew instinctually it was time to leave this haven of healing and as if responding to the same bell they both rose to make their way back onto the pathway through the trees.

"Come on Stella we are going on a treasure hunt. There's more to discover here before your return to earth, it's time to reconnect your memory with the seeds that you left in place. The seeds you unconsciously activated to transverse the challenges that beset human life."

Treasure Hunt

Even with her usual short strides she was well able to keep up with Yakazan who still appeared to get from one place to another by gliding. Looking ahead, the colour she could see left her with the impression that she was walking into a living kaleidoscope which curiously had stereo surround sound.

"Stella, stop looking for an orchestra, there isn't one hidden behind the trees. That sound you are now tuning into is the sound of delight, of fun and sometimes the twinkling sound of light or you may say tinkling. You have never complained about the tinnitus you experience on earth because there is a part of you that instinctively knew you were tuning into home and the vibrations throughout the inner planes.'

Stella was so excited to have something she had perceived to be true, for her, being affirmed. Whenever suggestions were made to her about the various treatments available, she always told others that the tinnitus didn't bother her as she *was listening to the choirs of Angels.'* She could now add 'tinkling of the fairies' to that statement.

Stella slowed her steps as they entered a grove of trees where the space was overflowing with circles within circles of bluebells, snowdrops and primroses. The air was filled with a sweet fragrance which carried whispers of words she couldn't quite catch before her attention was drawn to the cluster of pulsating primroses. The gentle sway of the flowers formed a natural corridor which allowed Stella to make her way to this vibrant yellow cluster. Going by instinct she eased herself into a kneeling position and reached into this cluster to retrieve the source of the pulsation, a light filled Citrine crystal. Snippets of conversations from long ago flowed through her mind as she held and gazed at this crystal and only stopped listening to them when the earlier whispers fused with the snippets to reveal the name of the energetic quality, she had infused into it. Although knowing Yakazan could hear her thoughts she excitedly voiced her discovery.

"I remember! This seed is Courage, and I can recall some of your words of counsel and encouragement to place it here for me to activate when needed. They were wise words then as are your words now."

"Stella what feels like long ago to you seems like yesterday for me. You were excited about your imminent earthbound adventure. When you infused this crystal seed with courage, I don't think you fully appreciated how much courage you would need. And before you incarnated, and something I mentioned earlier and is worth saying again, we did discuss the necessity of your forgetting your existence here. For here is where you experienced cooperation, joy, pure love, light and living with an innate knowing of being connected to the Creator's Universe. And if you left here retaining all that knowledge, you would never have been able to keep both feet on Mother Earth in order to progress through early and then the later years of your life cycle as a human. The forgetting enabled you to lower your natural high vibrations in order to adopt and adapt to earth's much denser energy. Your decision to go and leave the energetic vibrations you knew to those unknown to you was your first act of Courage. That goes not only for you Stella but is the same for every star seed and light-worker scattered throughout the Universe and those from other galaxies who choose to incarnate on Mother Earth."

Stella did understand but couldn't hold back the comment. "It may have been necessary but also rather sad not only for me but also for others that we had to forget all that we had left."

"Perhaps it will help Stella, if you focus on the joy of remembering now. Star seeds and light workers who make their way to Mother Earth are choosing to be a part of her healing and transformation. And in order to support her, that same healing and transformation needed to be part of your own earth walks. On your arrival Stella if you had continued to remember and kept one foot here that would have negated your lived human experiences and all you had set out to learn. Although I keep stressing that you will remember your time here now. When you return to your usual day to day experiences and challenges your human self will continue to see saw between forgetting and remembering. That's simply a part of life on earth. Eventually you will begin observing that you are making great strides in remembering while honouring what you set out to achieve."

Harsh, was one word that Stella thought could be used to describe the human condition as she thought of how her physical body had acted like a sponge absorbing her vulnerabilities, doubts and fears. The ability to see and do things differently had creeped in slowly, but before she'd became aware of what she was doing to herself she'd carried the effects of all that she had absorbed within her cells and organs of her human form. With consequences also being felt in her energetic mental, emotional bodies and chakra system. Yes, it did take courage she thought to seek out knowledge, step up, recognise and take responsibility for the times that her earth life in no way reflected one that was self-nourishing, and joy filled.

Stella had tried to be a really good daughter, wife, mother and friend but found herself thinking of the times she had fallen into playing the role of the victim, of not measuring up or being good enough and giving her power away to others believing what they said about her rather than what was true. Gratitude and astonishment didn't seem potent enough words to describe how she was feeling in that moment, but they were the only words she could muster. Yes, she was grateful that her crystal seed had activated even without her knowing it and astonished that when activated, it had been the agent of change to help her reshape her life. It is what encouraged her to begin to view herself differently and guided her to see clearly that she needed to cease denying the effects of playing the victim role she had cast for herself. Helping her to realise that role she'd cast herself in was based on the untrue opinions of others and society expectations.

It settled gently within her that this was indeed a life changing and valuable gift she'd left in place for herself. After her abridged life review, she was beyond thankful that courage had given her the boost, when needed, to follow through and release those untruths and so much more. *It was a gift she thought that kept on giving,* always guiding her towards higher vibrations of light, love and joy.

Moving her away from her previous normal to begin living what was natural.

"Your thoughts Stella are insightful. Courage has been and continues to be a treasured gift you gave to yourself. Your need to use this gift, and your life experiences may suggest otherwise, but you were always wrapped in the universal language of light and love. There's another aspect of courage at play here too as you also knew, before you left, it could take a lot of earth years for you to remember this, if at all."

For a moment there was no need for words between them, Stella actually felt as though she was breathing in Yakazan's love and compassion and as she looked towards her, she was surprised to witness Yakazan's shape shift into a light blue sapphire orb which floated to a stop in front of the middle of her forehead activating her third eye chakra. As she looked into the orb, she could still clearly see Yakazan's radiant features and hear her thoughts.

"Stella each time you activated your seed of courage we all rejoiced, and it strengthened our energetic connection, and we honoured the courage it took for you explore, release and rebuild yourself. Each occasion moving you into more light, joy and remembering. Come on Stella, are you ready and willing to follow where I lead? There are more memory seeds waiting to reconnect with a conscious you."

Trail of Fairy Dust

Smiling, Stella found she could stand with as much ease as it had been to previously kneel and there was a frisson of excitement in the air as she moved to join and follow Yakazan's orb form. As soon as they set off on this new pathway, they were immediately joined by numerous colourful orbs combining to create a welcome radiance. The purpose for their company was soon obvious when Stella, looking up, noticed that the natural light sources were blocked by a dense tree canopy. The light the orbs generated enabled her to move forward with confidence making it possible for her to see the colour and movement surrounding her. It also soon became clear how fortunate she was to have this extra light as the path snaked around trees and shrubs of different sizes. Both were filled with an impressive display of blossoms providing safe landing places for the countless multicoloured dragonflies. Glancing to the pathways' surface she noticed with great delight that the light enabled her to see that she was walking on a trail of bright, shining fairy dust.

As the path began to straighten Stella could just make out tiny specks of rubies which added sparkle to the trail of fairy dust she was following until it eventually came to an end at the wide base of a magnificent tree. Taking another look around her it seemed to Stella that she had been walking through the pages of the picture book she had often read to her granddaughter. She smiled at this memory before returning her attention to the tree, noticing that at its base the golden well like structure that nestled between delicate ferns was filled to the brim with fairy dust.

Moving her body with this new sense of ease Stella once again dropped without any awkwardness to her knees. Reaching out to pick up handfuls of fairy dust, she noticed as it slipped through her fingers the residual of the specks of rubies coated her fingers to a glowing red. Pleasure and joy filled her as she continued to scoop the grains of fairy dust. Hearing Yakazan's chuckles added to her delight.

"Stella, you planted one ruby before you poured yourself into a human body. These specks that are bringing you such delight originate from that single ruby. They increased in volume each time you activated the need of the energy you infused in it. Can you recall the quality and energy you infused it with?"

The answer needed no lengthy pondering and flowed quickly into her mind.

"For something to multiply so much, my heart tells me this is the seed of Willingness. It has indeed been a much used and powerful force in my life. I must have somehow known without knowing the role my ruby would play in my life and that I always needed to first be willing before setting out to make positive changes in my life. And wonders of wonders it is also my birthstone!"

"Yes, Stella Earth life can be filled with so many obstacles and I have heard your thoughts comparing willingness to a muscle that requires developing and strengthening. Much like the weightlifter in those thoughts of yours, that trains to be able to lift heavier weights or a ballet dancer whose repeated practice develops advanced skills. Then there's all those muscle repetitions stored in your neurological system when you learnt to drive a car. Humans have an amazing capacity to learn through repetition, but I say this without any judgement, just an observation, that unfortunately humans can use their brain's function against themselves."

Stella well understood Yakazan's comment.

"Thanks, Yakazan, I don't feel judged, and I am aware of how easy it is to fall into repetitive patterns of negative self-talk and beliefs."

Yakazan had more to add to her earlier comments. "Humans often play the game of 'Thought Ping Pong'. I see a puzzled look on your face Stella. Think for a moment where your thoughts land. Let's call it an original thought that pops into your brain or call it mind if you prefer. What do you the thinker do with it? I am not aiming this just at you Stella, but you will have experienced what I am speaking of."

"Well, Yakazan you have captured my attention, and I am with you so far."

"Let's backtrack to when the thought arrives, which is when the game of Ping Pong starts. Instead of simply being present with the thought, the thinker may decide it's a negative one. Then that kicks off the tendency or need to validate the negative thought with numerous memories of negative experiences. The Ping Pong ball can also head towards the creation of a positive thought that then connects the thinker to positive experiences. Neither is right nor wrong but in both cases the thinker is not in the present moment. Humans are very clever at being Ping Pong balls. And are just as clever, when they know how to cease this game. Which happens when the thought is acknowledged by the thinker who stays present with it, not in the past nor the future. The act of being present then allows for any required action or healing and transformation to take place."

"I get it Yakazan! And yes, that has been a game I have played well."

Stella lapsed into silence absorbing Yakazan's words then began to contemplate her adventure here. So far it felt like being in a room filled with people you have only heard about but were now able to put names to previously unknown faces. This was also an opportunity to add more to her life review.

She resonated with being a ping pong ball, it had taken her to times of regurgitating negative thought patterns and experiences. Even knowing how that habit could undermine any foundations she was trying to build to live a better version of herself, the need to do so would sometimes overwhelm her. Fortunately, when she became aware that her foundations were rocky that sense of teetering would guide her, like a map, back to the user-friendly self-beliefs that were evolving within her.

Continuing to put names to her experiences and life as a ball she recognised and owned, how her seed of courage had fueled her willingness to explore and flush out at their roots the detrimental effects of negative thought patterns on her mental, emotional and physical health.

She smiled while recalling that she had travelled many paths seeking to build new foundations for her physical and spiritual adventures. As this review continued to unfold, she thought about the path that directed her towards loving herself for who she was. Not a self-love that was only valid if others loved her. This path also included releasing any despair that she wasn't worth loving. Which enabled her to step out of the box others had put her in and forge new paths that were best for her. Self-love was worth staying present with and a good plan to put into action.

Her glowing red hands were emitting a vibrant energy and standing without any effort she brought them to rest in front of her face which caused more memories and feelings to rush through her. She was now remembering that in the rebuilding of her foundations she had been confused and burdened by how many limiting beliefs she had needed to overcome.

"My goodness Yakazan" came out as a long sigh." I feel like I should be singing the song 'Here I Go Again 'as more negative thoughts are springing up about the many times that I have been painfully embarrassed by some of the mistakes I have made along the way. Speaking out of turn, saying the wrong thing or not saying anything at all. Cringe worthy moments when I thought I was acting from right thinking when I clearly wasn't. Times when I really had to dig deep for the courage and willingness to recapture the joy instead of going into struggle.

As if from a distance she could hear Yakazan calling her.

"Stella don't go getting stuck in that human need to dissect and analyse everything. Stay present and detach yourself from those thoughts. Remember the ball and yes, you experienced low points, but you became adept at flexing your seed of willingness like that muscle metaphor you relate to. You continued to gather your courage to step past limiting beliefs and shifted so many perceptions while seeking clarity. It all was how it was. Which brings you to this moment in time. Put the ping pong ball aside it's part of a road that you no longer need to go down. Be willing now to believe you have released yourself from that particular game and road to fly among the stars. We have and I loved it when we did."

Sensing the sapphire orb near her ear Stella was filled with an immense joy hearing Yakazan's words as she remembered that she had lived nearly four decades of earth years, before she had set her course to learn, awaken and expand her awareness through joy, not suffering.

"And besides that, Stella" Yakazan's voice broke through her thoughts, "you had to live without your fairy wings. You needed to lower your energy to such a density to maintain your presence on earth. Your wings would have taken you lightly to pathways of the highest vibration. Instead, your human self through trial and error found the paths that encouraged the raising of your physical and spiritual vibration. Here your ruby seed of willingness was constantly glowing and multiplying as you sought to unload the heavy burdens of false beliefs and fears. Which led to some of those miscreation's. The occasions when you surrendered those burdens, you lightened up your earthly vibrations and you transformed to being less dense. Embracing the higher vibrations and energies of self-love and joy helped too as they animated your human body. And continue to do so."

Like a laser beam Stella focused on the word miscreation. That was a perfect word she thought to describe mistakes. Both words were simply earth life choices to try out ideas to see if they work or not. The lived experience of them not working out had provided her with wonderful opportunities to recreate and choose again. With these thoughts in her mind, she was able to view her lived experience on earth as unfolding on a playground. And everything that she was doing or being, created that life.

The ball was and always had been in her court for healing and transformation. It seemed appropriate to rub her hands together and in doing so she felt an intense generation of heat. She valued having this time to reflect and was indebted to willingness for being a part of the mantle she wore. Taking some deep cleansing breaths, she was happy to see the orbs still hovering in the area, her eyes sought the sapphire orb only to see that once again Yakazan had returned to her earlier form. This time her wings were more noticeable and brighter.

"Come on Stella although time doesn't mean much here, it is starting to pass on earth. Let's go now and find your wings."

Fairy Wings

Following Yakazan it seemed to only take a few steps to leave the previous path and move forward to another path, that needed no other lights as they left the canopy of trees behind and had them heading towards yet another different landscape. *They were entering wonderland* was Stella's first thought because the sight that greeted her of a mixture of the whitest and coarsest grains of sands she'd ever seen.

This spectacular area was further divided into geometrical patterns formed by small green leafy informal hedges. Her eyes had no trouble looking at the brilliant sparkle of the sand. Back on earth such brightness would have her reaching for her sunglasses, but here she could absorb the dazzling light and easily see the steppingstones set in place to guide her across this open area. She was able to make her way across the stones with an easy stride and could clearly hear an audible sigh of welcome when her foot made contact on each stone. *Talking stones*, she thought and was more curious about what was to come next rather than surprised by them.

Ahead she noticed the stones were also taking them through a clear running stream and once across, Yakazan was guiding her towards a white crystal garden bench. The tree close by cast no shade and appeared to be continually changing colour as various butterflies coming and going alighted on the branches. Once she was seated next to Yakazan, Stella closed her eyes and began to get an inkling of what she was about to rediscover. The tingling sensation flowing throughout her body was familiar as one she'd experienced each time she trusted her own abilities and what actions to take or who to interact with. The clarity she felt on such occasions was reflected in her present bright surroundings and was the reward for trusting herself. For her trust and clarity often walked hand in hand.

Before becoming totally lost in her thoughts she opened her eyes marveling once more at the lack of need to shield her eyes from the brightness surrounding her. Then a thought struck her, she had set off on her walk wearing her sunglasses, but like her shoes, were absent. Interestingly she wasn't curious about their fate.

Her inkling was confirmed by Yakazan's soft whisper.

"Stella, this is the Trust Garden."

She sensed immediately that soft, hushed whispers were suited to this setting. Louder voices would be so out of place.

"And now it's my turn to say 'oh my goodness' about what I can only describe as what feels like a coin being flipped around in your head. Maybe it will help to talk about it here where Trust surrounds us."

Responding in kind to Yakazan's whispers she quietly began to form words from the memories that were indeed flipping like a coin, similar to the ball from a positive, upside then back again to the down or negative one. Apparently, there were still some things she needed to review. But this time she was doing so with a sense of detachment.

"Yakazan on the upside I can say that my life has begun to reflect the trust that I have been nurturing through simply believing in myself and in my abilities and healing gifts. I learnt to move away from those that energetically drain me, or situations that didn't resonate with my wellbeing, or what is true for me. It did take a lot of that courage and willingness to give myself permission to do so. But once I realised that moving away was not about judging wrongness within myself or another. It became natural to test the waters and only wade into what was best for me."

"And what of the downside you keep flipping to Stella? On that side you once wore a mask of false confidence that fooled many. The one you hid all your fears and insecurities behind."

"Trust you Yakazan, excuse the pun, to take my memories there. But then again, every coin has two sides. Rather like the ping pong ball you spoke of that goes back and forth. Plus, along the way I learnt that revealing and acknowledging my vulnerabilities plays a big part in being real. Yes, I did believe a lot of falsehoods about myself along with those I allowed others to project onto me via their own insecurities. Difficult not to feel betrayed when someone you trust does so and spreads untruths about you.

The mask stayed firmly in place as I thought I needed to at least appear confident, be a people pleaser and agree with the beliefs and opinions of others.

When understanding finally dawned of how my own behaviour was actually harming my possibility for any future personal growth, I began to develop a natural inner confidence which slowly started to replace the false one. It took time but as the mask slipped away, I could clearly see how the beliefs of others which I supported were often the direct opposite of my own and that I no longer needed to agree with others for the sake of peace. As I recall these memories, I can only be grateful for the downside which led me to the upside and that I chose to stop living and playing this superficial fear-based game."

Stella didn't feel the need utter any more words. The coin had stopped flipping and as it came to a rest, she reminded herself that she knew Trust's signature well for it always turned up with tingling and joyful sensations. She mentally crossed her fingers that when what ever felt right for her was tested in situations or by the opinions of others she would continue to listen and be guided by her gut instincts. They were the barometer she could rely on to discern if something resonated in her best interests or not.

"Ahh Stella," Yakazan continued in her soothing soft tone "your human self needed to experience a lack of esteem and confidence coupled with the challenges of feeling disempowered. You needed to live through the lessons you set in place for yourself which included that sense that there's something wrong with you and that from another's perspective you couldn't seem to do or say the right thing. Stella, you brought splendid teachers into your life to aid you. You created many learning opportunities. Experiencing the opposite of what was natural and inherent within you became the gift that eventually led you to how real trust felt for you. That awareness and accompanying sensations guided you to trust your own abilities and discern where life situations and people reflected your joy and how to avoid what would diminish it. Trust opened you to receive everything you needed to resolve and evolve.

Again, we rejoiced when you surrendered all that was untrue about yourself as you allowed the brightness and clarity of trust to replace the cloudiness of untruths and your miscreations. This garden reflects the quality of clarity that became and remains a part of your new mindset. That's why you can gaze into its dazzling light without needing to glance away.

I think I also need to add as well using your personal barometer to build self-trust and align with all aspects of yourself, your truth, will be a topic you revisit many times. No doubt there will more trust conversations in your future and with me as well. In your human form you will continue to experience fluctuations in your levels of trust."

Stella had often pondered on the puzzle pieces of her life and how finding some of those pieces served to highlight that there were other pieces waiting to be found. Being here with Yakazan and especially in the trust garden it felt like a few more pieces of the puzzle were slipping into place and was undaunted by the fact that there would be more to come. Human life was in no way static it was filled with ups and downs. And yes, she thought she had experienced those fluctuations Yakazan spoke of. One moment Trust was firmly anchored in her everyday reality and yet could quickly wane when in situations that triggered old beliefs to resurface. One thing she knew required no puzzling over was to continue her regular visits to her personal Crystal Pyramid. For the umpteenth time she reminded herself it was real. To have such a healing tool at her disposal along with the power of the Violet Flame brought with It an ongoing sense of comfort and joy rather than ones of failure for being there. *Being here Is real too, she thought.*

Which led her to asking while still whispering in this sacred space.

"I can sense that this garden has always been here, and I can grasp the fact that trust is the seed, but what did I leave in place to activate the processes for developing self-trust?"

Smiling, Yakazan turned to Stella with a twinkle in her eyes, "I am going to recite a poem you wrote so many earth years ago. I know the words well and have held them close in my own heart. I am certain you know the one I am referring to; can you recall the title?"

Sifting through the files in her mind Stella did remember and still whispering though that was getting harder the more excited she became. 'Yes, it was called 'What is Trust?"

Stella listened to Yakazan 's soothing voice softly reciting her own words to her.

"I asked a question?
I asked it with my head.
And not my heart.
My heart knows only trust.
It's like the gossamer.
Of fairy wings.
Flimsy in appearance
Yet you know they'll
Fly you way into the stars.
Take you far.
And you will not fall.
For in your heart
You know.
Trust and you will go far."

Grasping the message hidden in those words written long ago and without any need for further comments Stella made her way to the butterfly tree. Nestled on the lowest branch she instantly recognised her gossamer fairy wings. Tears of overwhelming and indescribable joy flowed down her face as she gingerly and reverently reached out to touch them while at the same time she was filled with the wonder of knowing how they had continued to activate and support her earth journey, instinctively knowing, when her need for moments of trust and clarity had been great.

With that first touch her wings magnetized to her hands while she drank in their beauty.

Her gossamer wings glistened with various shades of iridescent blue deepening as layers upon layer came together forming a natural centre. Speech was beyond her, all she was capable of was smiling as Yakazan took her wings from her hands and reverently affixed them to her thoracic spine.

The sensation of them fluttering and lengthening created more waves of joy and delight to flow through her body which she was noticing was getting lighter and lighter. In that moment the phrase 'lightness of being' made perfect sense to her.

Moving to her side Yakazan asked Stella to take her hand and to either say to herself or out loud.

"I can hover."

Stella was delighted to comply and, in a flash, found herself hovering over the trust garden. "Stella now say 'beam me up Scottie." This had Stella dissolving into laughter.

"What?" Laughed Yakazan "You doubted me when I said I was with you? That was the only part of that television show I enjoyed. Now say let's fly!"

Wonders of wonders she was flying without any hesitation and as she repeated to herself.

"I can do this." After several repetitions, Yakazan released her hand.

Together they soared above the tree canopy that had covered the path to her seed of Willingness. Then circled the flowers where she could see the cluster which enclosed her seed of Courage pulsating yellow vibrations into the air before moving onto gaining a bird's eye view of her own crystal pyramid healing chamber. She was surprised to see her sparkling white shoes outside the chamber along with her neatly folded sunglasses. That's where they got to, she thought. She hadn't really missed either of them.

Stella no longer felt like earth bound Stella. She was air, light and filled with bubbles of ecstatic joy. Bubbles that connected with the Sylphs as they flew over their part of this wondrous realm. She could make out their tall slender shapes which transformed to puffs of air taking on the shapes and colour of wing shaped clouds. Their intermittent puffs resonated within her as welcome hellos. Stella could also tune into Yazakan's delight and was able to hear her thoughts that expressed her pleasure for this time together. Some memories of times long past when they had journeyed to the stars and planets also filtered through her mind. But no thoughts or memories could detract from being present on this exhilarating, unforgettable and magical adventure.

They continued to fly over and through many different landscapes that all had movement and colour in common. What may have appeared busy on earth felt peaceful which filled the air she breathed and settled within her as she flew in and around as well as over. She knew she would never have enough adjectives to describe what she was experiencing in this moment of time nor the elation of stepping out of her usual human time.

As they circled around, Stella noticed the Trust Garden coming back into view which suggested to her that her flight was drawing to a close. Reaffirming in that moment that nothing and that included any further earth life challenges, could take away the sheer bliss of this momentous experience and knew with certainty that it would live on in the cells of her physical body and her memories. She was experiencing freedom as an energy not something found in an event or situation. Hovering for a few moments Yakazan took her hand again as they descended, landing smoothly and gently back at their starting place.

What About?

As her feet connected with the dazzling coarse sand Stella became aware of a current of light energy flowing down through the top of her head, rushing through her body and into her feet. She recognised that the purpose of this energy was to ground her and at the same time she felt her wings gracefully retracting. Looking around she was able to reconnect with the clarity of Trust ever-present in this garden.

"Come on Stella let's sit awhile," Yakazan broke into her thoughts and led her again to the crystal bench. "Stella, I can hear you mentally scratching your head and even though they are entering like gentle waves, questions are forming in your mind and now is the time to ask them."

Sitting quietly Stella started to gather those questions and even though she wished to stay quiet the mental scratching was becoming a bit annoying. *But where to start,* she thought and before she spoke, she took in a deep breath letting it out on a long sigh that was accompanied by an 'okay'.

Taking in another breath she began. "When I woke up this morning, I would never have envisaged having this experience and to know it's all true fills me with tremendous excitement. I fully accept I planted the seeds of Courage, Willingness and Trust but, and this has got me scratching my human head didn't I also need to plant love, light and joy?"

Stella then felt that while she was on a roll adding. "And what about wisdom, forgiveness and peace?"

Looking at Yakazan and noticing that beatific smile she had become used to seeing on her face she was surprised when she asked, "how's the itch?"

"Why gone but replaced by curiosity!" Checking in Stella was able to discern that her mind had settled then with a burst of knowing she knew the answers to her own question.

"One of those lightbulb moments you enjoy Stella!" She heard Yakazan comment.

"Yes indeed! I have been using the word rebuild, and I now think a more appropriate word would be redefine. My foundations were never teetering, as I believed, they were always supported by the bedrock of love, light and joy, along with everything I needed to continue evolving on my earthly spiritual path and wherever those paths may still take me. This hasn't anything to do with my age now or the idea of being at a crossroad. While living through the challenges of this earthly journey, I have always been drawing this truth to me."

"What a gift you are Stella to all of us in this realm, beyond and to those on earth," she heard the smile in Yakazan's words. "Along with the fairies who maintained their original form you spread seeds of love and peace throughout Mother Earth. They had already been germinated within you and the more you produced the more you had to spread and share.

Stella every time you exercised your Courage, Willingness and Trust you rose above those human challenges, especially the illusionary thoughts of worthlessness or wrongness. You learnt to use the power of the illusion to guide you to the truth that you were the very opposite of such thoughts. At those times your human self was able to feel the energy of love, embrace self-love and then experience the states of being joy, happiness, compassion and so much more that comes along with being love. Wisdom was already at play as you were able to explore, release and yes redefine is a better word to describe your evolution. Peace which was ever present also helped you return to a state of feeling balanced and guide you to seek and find the tranquility of being in harmony with nature."

Sitting quietly, Stella was absorbing all Yakazan's words which confirmed she was already what she had always been striving to be. And was only too happy for Yakazan to continue.

"I witnessed Stella how you were able to raise your vibrations and as you did so you became less dense and more able to contain higher levels of light and then radiate it. That inner light continues to grow in you and guides you and it signals you when you are out of balance or diving into self-doubt. Love brings with it all the qualities humans keep striving for and that's the same for peace just as you have experienced when you felt balanced and in harmony within yourself, others and the world around you."

Breathing deeply again the air seemed even fresher as Yakazan's words settled within her.

Giving herself a moment to absorb Yakazan's words she went on to add her own comments to this present discussion.

"I could also think of it this way. When I embody love it's like a package deal that brings along with it joy, compassion, kindness, gratitude and so much more. It's the same for Peace and all the qualities that accompany that state of being. I can hear the words of a very old song playing in my head 'you can't have one without the other."

Then she realised the reverse of that is also true. The package deal of fear can also bring with it anger, frustration doubts and judgements. Hearing Stella's thoughts Yakazan directed her to fully appreciate her power of choice and her ability to forgive herself.

"Stella, you have made a practice out of self-forgiveness and each time you forgave yourself for ever having the need to create the situations that caused you pain, you were able to view them as opportunities to heal what needed healing within you. What you perceived as opportunities offered you the chance to release any others involved from any judgement, and it became a time for you to give joy and love back to yourself. Isn't that how you think of it?"

"Yes, Yakazan forgiveness in that sense is for giving back to myself."

"And Stella, each time you raised your vibration in that way. It was like opening the treasure chest within you for everything you needed to come forth."

Stella could feel another question forming and before she could voice it Yakazan continued. "There will be periods again when you forget but there will also be lots of reminders. One could be as simple as noticing a newly blossomed flower or watching a bird in flight. Each can trigger a remembering which is only ever a thought away. Your time here is like a software update. This connection will remain regardless of what you may be doing in any moment. Nothing or no one else can break it, only you can dilute it. Now please ask your question."

For a few moments Stella was content to be still and silent, there were so many layers to this adventure that she was trying to absorb. Before arriving here, she was questioning new paths she wished to follow if any? What changes could she make in her work role as a therapist that would both support her physically and fulfill her desire to assist others? She was becoming aware of the changes in her body. Did she still wish to work in those roles and if she did could she still create room in her life for fun, enjoyment and travel? She, fully understood what others meant when she heard them say after retiring 'I don't know how I had time to work.'

"Well, Yakazan here's my next question, one you have no doubt heard swirling around inside my head. Why now? And here's another. Why not years ago when in earth years I was a lot younger?"

With reverence Yakazan removed her wings and placed them back on the butterfly tree as she had now come to think of it. Silently she reached out to touch and connect with them once more and as she bade them farewell. She could still feel their presence like a hand between her shoulder blades, a sensation that she was very familiar with.

"A very good question Stella and worthy of an answer as uncomplicated as possible. In order to achieve that, it's time to visit the woman by the waterfall who caught your eye when you arrived. She has been waiting. Follow me we only need the sound of the water to guide us."

Liquid Light Woman

Leaving the clear white light of the Trust Garden behind Stella was happy to follow Yakazan and step into the landscape that her eyes had feasted on when she'd first come through the portal into this realm. The grass seemed greener if that was possible and the flowers were a spectacular array of colours. The air was filled with that fresh clean taste again and her eyes, now so well adjusted to being here, could see the perfume from the flowers vibrating into the air, before her gaze was again drawn to the healing pools. And visible once more by the larger pool and waterfall was the beautiful woman who Yakazan had earlier referred to as the Liquid Light Woman.

Her already heightened senses experienced a de ja vu moment as she made her way around the smaller pools and as she came closer the Liquid Light Woman remained in her beautiful woman form. When she spoke, her voice was melodious and created sparks of light and delight to flow through her.

"Welcome, Stella yes you now have more questions, and I will get to your 'why now?' soon but I can sense your intense curiosity about 'who I am?'. That is another thing to treasure about yourself Stella, your curiosity."

By now Stella had become so used to the exchange of thoughts between her and Yakazan that to also have this connection with the Liquid Light Woman seemed as natural as breathing.

"Come Stella before we resolve your curiosity let's get another view of the waterfall and go behind the curtain of water."

Stepping behind the waterfall was like stepping into a hall of mirrors. But ones that didn't distort. The rock formation which created the background and the shelf on which she now stood glistened with an astonishing intensity to create this mirrored effect. From this perspective the curtain of water resembled a beaded curtain made up of individual drops of dancing light interspersed with rainbow sprays. Wondering for a split second if glimpsing the presence of a Unicorn where she had previously been standing before slipping behind the waterfall was her imagination? But then she shook her head to chase that thought away as she wholeheartedly accepted that nothing in this experience was her imagination. The dictionary's definition of faith flashed through her mind 'complete trust or confidence in someone or something.' She remembered how puzzled she had felt by having the need to look that up a few days ago. In a moment of clarity, she realised she was finally trusting and fully embracing Yakazan's prior words, to accept and believe that none of this was her imagination.

"Ahhh Stella thank you for believing and never giving up faith on your Earth journey and for taking the offered hand and joining us here and staying present with all we wish to share. Yes, it does look like a beaded curtain even though it is a continuous stream of water and light. We also refer to it as the river of light that connects us all. Your Soul which is way bigger than your human form or bubble of biology lights you up and connects your sparkling drop to this river. And that's true for all humans not just a few."

It was taking Stella a few moments to adjust, and *bedazzled* was the word she thought described the myriad of sensations flowing through her physical body and beyond. Her oft repeated intentions for her physical and spiritual life to be under her soul's guidance was manifesting and becoming real in this moment.

The longing to listen and heed the voices of love, light and joy had always been with her. This Earth life she'd been living hadn't been one of one negative thought or situation after another. Unfortunately, those times were the ones that were easier to remember and cause her energy to contract. Thankfully there were also numerous times spent celebrating when she'd succeeded in experiencing the joy of love, and fortunately had become adept at noticing when worldly judgement, doubts and fearful voices were trying to creep in. It may have taken her years but at such times when they did make their presence felt, she had developed the habit of smiling to herself. What had helped her when fear showed up in one of its many disguises was her growing understanding that it was herself, no other, that was creating these opportunities to live her life in either fear or love. Or to put it another way. Fear often generated a state of contraction and sensations of being stuck or sucked into quicksand. While love promoted a state of expansion and created the sense of being a liberated and larger-than-life energy. Both extremes taught her the value of consistently choosing to grow through love into love.

"Since arriving here Stella you have been remembering what you already know and that mimics the purpose of your life on earth. To remember what you already know and guide others to remembering who they are as well. And that is what you have been doing and will continue to do so but this moment in time is just for you."

Excitement usually caused lots of thoughts to tumble through Stella's mind diverting her attention quickly from one subject or project to another. That tendency wasn't going to work in this instance because she needed to be fully present and listen to the words this beautiful woman of Liquid Light wished to convey.

"Stella much Divine wisdom and light is imprinted in all your cells. You planted your seeds, and they flourished as you grew. When your human self was in need they activated. They were never meant for one use only. I am adding to Yakazan's earlier words to emphasise, that unknown to you the more you activated them the potency and efficacy of your seeds continued to be replenished."

Even as Stella's eyes were alternating between drinking in the sight of the curtain of water and the shimmering effects of the Liquid Light woman, she was captivated by her words. They seemed to be sparkles of light themselves flowing with natural ease throughout her body.

"Stella for some time during your meditation practice and quest to gain even more self-awareness and knowledge you have been connecting to that bright spark of light which is your Soul. As aspects of you we have witnessed you visualising your soul as a multifaceted diamond within your heart chakra and then observed that when your attention was fully focused on that diamond it grew bigger and brighter able to reflect rays of pure light throughout your body and way beyond."

Again, the Liquid Light Woman emphasised. "Stella this is not your imagination, you have been able to experience your body fitting into your Soul's energy not the other way around. There will be an appropriate time in the future for you to explore more fully your place in the Universe as a multidimensional being. The time for such an exploration is not now, because you will need to return to your earthly experience soon. And in right timing one bit at a time, you will have even more understanding of how to live in and from your Soul's energy."

Stella could recount the times she felt frustrated or impatient when she wished to know everything at once. Unlike those occasions in this instance, she appreciated the value of being patient. Without the presence of frustration, she noticed the words floating through her mind all started with the letter A. Aspects, accept, attention, appropriate, appreciate and here comes another she chuckled to herself, activate then came another absorb. That last A word had her realise before trying to absorb more information she needed to appreciate this time and give it her attention in order to embrace and embody this incredible experience. One that without any doubt carried the potential to continue to change the landscape of her thoughts about her spiritual and physical life.

The Liquid Light woman's words became even more melodious as Stella brought her attention back to her discourse.

"Stella, when you overcame your initial hesitancy and placed your hand in the proffered hand of light, you then easily accepted and connected with Yakazan. This joining of hands stimulated some memories to rise to the surface and their truth sat comfortably with you. And I know it's not too much of a reach for you to accept that your physical body for some time has had the ability to hold higher vibrations of light, love and joy which in turn reflects your Soul's pure essence. Sometimes your human self can often have moments of forgetfulness and find it hard to believe that the body you inhabit is also your vehicle of joy with the capacity to radiate that light and joy to others. We know when the forgetting passes you get back on track seeking to express this through your thought processes and words in everyday life."

Tears were forming in Stella's eyes in response to the truth on hearing these words. And floating through her mind were words she'd often think after making deep connections whether it be for a moment or maybe longer, he or she was a 'beautiful soul.' Yes, she thought in wonder you can notice the Soul as a radiating presence that has an impact seen or unseen. She thought of the countless times that it had been said to her 'let your light shine.' What a wonderful world it would be she mused if everyone *let their light shine.*

"Stella, you have indeed been letting your light shine and as you step into a more intense, purer light and love energy you will return to Mother Earth walking with a lighter step. Through simply being yourself, you will be a healing presence for others and the world. Notice I said being not doing. Let all your concerns about being at a crossroads go. There really isn't anything you need to do but what will be new for you is to live your life unconcerned about the opinions of others about what you could or should do. Perhaps think of it this way Stella, your life is not about what you need to do but where you need to act. Stay open to wisdom and knowledge, be love in action for yourself first then others. Act only on what brings joy into your life. Apply Trust and trust that wisdom, knowledge, love and joy will make a difference in your everyday reality. There will be a natural flow on effect that will benefit others."

The Liquid Light Woman took hold of Stella's right hand, Yakazen her left, and without any warning but with a delightful outcome they propelled her through the curtain of water into the pool beyond. Laughing Stella rose to the surface and was astounded by the cleansing and healing effect of the water. Floating in this buoyant and pure water was so blissful before feeling drawn to make her way across to the side of the pool to sit with Yakazan and the Liquid Light Woman on another rock that doubled as a seat. As she approached Stella was awed by the sight of an effervescence glow of changing colours surrounding them. Then noticed that it also encompassed her.

Yakazan's voice crept gently into Stella's sense of bliss and wonder.

"Stella now is the time to ask your question."

So much had happened since Stella had first asked her question 'why now?.' There was a phrase floating through her mind a voice is silent unless it is heard, hearing it Stella gathered the sensations and thoughts created from what she had just experienced before taking a deep breath and exhaling on a sigh she asked it again.

"Why now?" she repeated. "I have lived many earth years. I acknowledge that I have created and passed through painful and joyful experiences on my earth walk. I have had many glimpses of myself as an expanded energy, consciously seeking and gaining the understanding that I am more than my physical body I have played with the idea without any proof that I am a fairy. So why not then on the many paths I followed or when I was younger?"

With one of her beautiful smiles Yakazan's gentle tones soothed and calmed any confusion that accompanied her questions before the Liquid Light Woman continued.

"Ahhh Stella, thank you and yes, it's hard to hear a silent voice. Actions can be interpreted, and assumptions made but you are ready, and it is time now to find other ways for your voice to be heard. Why now? At this stage of your earth life, you are more flexible and willing to go with the flow. You have a freedom that you didn't always allow when you consciously or unconsciously put constraints on the use of your time. You have the understanding now that time doesn't do anything, you choose how to use your time."

This was making sense Stella thought as the melodious voice of the Liquid Light Woman added more to her answer.

"Stella, your human personality exudes a youthful and vital energy that is noticed by many despite those many earth years you talk about. But what is also noticed and appreciated and listened to is your wisdom. Your human age in fact commands respect. Those that hear you know that you are not an empty vessel preaching platitudes. There is a term 'walk your talk' that is bandied about on Mother Earth and that is what you do so admirably. When you share words or ideas with another, they are credible along with your counsel that you only speak what is true for you and is not necessarily what is true for another. Your words act as a trigger that leads them to their own truth. Without even knowing it or even needing to know it you have done that repeatedly.

Again, why now?

Being here awake has hastened your remembering. On earth you were already beginning to do so. We encourage you to stay open to receiving more insights which will not only further enrich your life but assist you in maintaining your connection to your inner wisdom. When you value this wisdom your light and authenticity will shine through when you share what resonates with you. Trusting yourself and your voice will mirror or show the way for others to continue to explore their own treasure chests."

Stella heard their unspoken thoughts to immerse herself in the pool again and before slipping into the water, she noticed that the bottom of the pool was lined with crystals of different shapes and colours. Alternately diving below the surface and floating Stella laughed delightedly each time the colour of the water changed. The vibration of each shift seeped into every cell of her body. She was *the water and a drop at the same time* she thought, before experiencing her body being filled with love, joy, light, sheer bliss and wonder. Then finally pure contentment.

Gradually different sounds penetrated her awareness. At first, she thought her head was filled with the buzz of all the spoken words then her ears picked up the tone of a bell. Her senses were on alert for yet another change and knew in that instant that it was time to leave and return to the retreat.

Her exit from the pool was achieved with a grace that was not of her doing. Effervescent colours continued to surround her as her physical body and retreat clothes took form again. Feeling buoyed by love and exquisite joy she made her way to her now dazzling white shoes and sunglasses which had magically made their appearance near the pool. Stepping into them she expected to feel sad but instead was filled with gratitude as she looked around committing all the wonder around her to memory and then wasn't the least bit surprised as she watched the shapes and colours that had welcomed her integrate and blend. The outcome of that merging caused some colours to intensify and flash which also created audible waves of sound oscillating at different frequencies that harmonised rather than creating any discord.

Stella felt rather than saw the Liquid Light Woman move closer as she listened to the melodious voice, she had become used to.

"You are amazing Stella you have so easily absorbed this perceptional shift. When you came through the portal into this dimension what you observed brought you great joy and delight and was vital to your remembering. Once the word Fairy had been uttered your perception responded to the set images you held in your mind of what this world would look like. Humans do the same when Angels are mentioned your mind is filled with forms and wings rather than their reality of existing as energetic vibrations, rather colourful perhaps but as pure energy.

The fact that Humans hold onto these images, giving the formless form, doesn't make them less real."

With the evidence in front of her there was no room for any doubt. Stella was finally moving beyond dismissing the word imagine as creating something that isn't real. To understanding the power of imagination and its role in how to create or re imagine her own life on Earth.

The Liquid Light Woman's softly spoken words further assured her.

"Stella, your time here has raised your vibrations and increased the speed of your natural sight enabling you to see the pure energy that exists beyond the shapes and forms you see in your everyday life. I am returning to the vibrations of the ninth dimension, my energetic home, knowing that when it's an appropriate part of your growth cycle you will visit me there."

The next few moments were charged with emotions that needed no words and as Stella bowed her head in awe and gratitude her sensory awareness discerned the departure of the Liquid Light Woman. Returning her gaze to Yakazan's beautiful and glorious form she once again experienced the sensation of her hand being held as she heard Yakazan's soothing voice imparting some final words of encouragement.

"Stella wield the power of your imagination wisely for this will determine how you live your life. When you accept your role in all your creations therein lies the superpower you have in the power to choose."

Allowing those words to sink in Yakazan continued.

"Take a deep breath Stella, then close your eyes and visualise the walking path you first set out on. When I say jump you will once more experience the sense of flying but you will soon find your feet back on Mother Earth and follow the sound of the bell. Jump Stella jump!"

CASSIE
The Fourth Day

Despite the everyday challenges of life Cassie liked to think that she and Josh were living the concept known as the fourth day. She had read about the term being applied to the experience of settling back into everyday life after the highs of life-changing events or workshops. For them it was Crow's three-day Angelic retreat. Some of those articles had discussed the realities of the participants incorporating and applying any of their newly learnt philosophies and life skills in their daily routines. Some blossomed and had advanced further along their chosen paths while others faltered unable to integrate new ideas or even see their benefit.

Cassie knew or hoped that both herself and Josh fell into the blossoming category. They had gained so much on their memorable retreat. Gone was any lingering fear of discussing issues or differing point of views that may have in the past caused any upset. She often heard Stella's words running through her mind like a rhythmic poem especially focusing on the final question'... What sort of life am I sentencing myself to?

Thinking of Stella always bought a smile to her face. Their friendship had grown to such an extent that they were often included in Stella's family gatherings. Her children and grandchildren were delightful people. They treasured the time when they had more one on one time with Stella and a bonus was the deep friendship that was developing between Josh and Stella's husband Barry.

With Josh on the sidelines cheering her on she had completed her Naturopathy course. With that degree framed and proudly hanging on the wall in her treatment space she was able to expand the range of services available to her existing and to any future clients.

She loved working with others and watching the improvements in their health. One of Stella's gems of advice was not to invest in the outcome that a client's recovery was solely dependent on her. Acting on that welcome advice she set her intention 'to attract clients that prized good health, and ones that would play an active role in achieving the goals they had set for themselves.' A rather lengthy one but in a nutshell attracting and treating clients that were committed to improving their own health.

And she was able to breathe a grateful sigh of relief that if the steady flow and increase in the clients seeking her services was any indication there were many in alignment with her intentions. She was filled with joy and remained in awe of being able to keep fulfilling her dream to be of service to others in this manner.

Her path had finally meandered back to her and Josh's desire for a family and they had just passed the seventh month of her pregnancy. According to her Doctor and her own intuition this pregnancy was proceeding well. In fact, she had never felt better and her clients, if the gifts were a good sign, rather than feel abandoned by the fact that she would need to take some time off, were all excited and supportive about this precious time in her life.

It was nice though to have an afternoon off and take time to sit overlooking the garden that they had spent many hours creating. Profusion and smells of both flowers and herbs took her on a trip down memory lane and she could once again picture herself during those final hours of the retreat.

One particular memory visited her often and she found herself, once more recalling the concern she'd felt about Stella's lack of appearance at the final lunch of the retreat. Joining in with the lively lunchtime discussions she had been able to put that concern aside only to have it resurface when lunch had been cleared away and the washing up done. She had even made a mug of Stella's favourite herbal tea and put it in a safe place for her. The other participants were gathering their notebooks and starting to make their way back to the main meeting room.

While still mystified by Crow's earlier enigmatic smile she sought her out to again voice her concern. Crow assured her that Stella was okay then gave her the bell to summon any stragglers to the afternoon sessions asking her to ring it through the corridors then go out into the garden and put some umph into ringing it. Carrying out Crow's wishes she had made her way through the corridors before making her way along the verandah into the garden where she put an extra surge of energy into sounding that bell.

Crow slipped quietly to her side as she bought the ringing to an end, and she was startled to see Stella coming along the track but to be more exact she noticed stunning glowing colours before she recognised Stella's physical form. Placing the bell down she closed her eyes and looked again. Stella resembled a hologram, her physical form flicking in and out of reality. And was that a Unicorn guiding her? Looking to Crow she remembered asking her "am I really seeing this?"

There was that smile again with Crow nodding her head while commenting.

"Cassie remember those words 'seeing is believing.' Yes, you can believe what you are seeing. Please go and ask my assistant to start a drumming circle, that will raise the energy and wake everyone up after lunch. I am going to welcome Stella and go to her room with her. Can you bring that cup of tea that you so lovingly made for her? And Cassie, Stella has been on a marvelous adventure, she's fine, see even the guidance of the Unicorn is no longer required and has returned to its home in the seventh dimension."

To Cassie it had seemed as though she had wings on her feet as she carried out Crow's bidding. Entering Stella's room felt like walking into a sacred space, and she could immediately sense the energetic waves emanating from Stella's physical form. She would forever remember the magical glow that enveloped both her and Crow and, in her mind's eye, continued to see Stella's sparkling eyes and even brighter smile before speaking in a soft yet clear voice.

"Thank you to you both your presence has anchored me. The sensation of being untethered has passed. Have no concern I feel wonderful."

Then looking at them both with a grin from ear-to-ear Stella shared a startling snippet of her journey, well it was startling for her, they were words she had mulled over many times.

"I may be starting towards the end but there will come a time when I can share more of my adventure. But it's enough to say I have some clear answers. I started out at the beginning of this weekend feeling rather lost and confused. I had that image that I shared with you Cassie and one I couldn't shake of standing at a crossroad wondering which road to take. Such indecisiveness about what I could or should be doing. In that state it was easy to ignore and avoid paying attention to another struggle that was taking place within me."

Stella maintained eye contact with them both as she stopped to draw in some more slow deep breaths then seemed to find the words she was looking for before continuing.

"When I use the word struggle, I am not referring to the struggle between good or bad, light or darkness. Or the struggle between truth and illusions. I can now acknowledge that before coming on this retreat, along with the sense of lostness the struggle that had been going on within me was whether I reject what I sense and have been told as fanciful thinking or accept and love my fairy origin. I am happy to report that the struggle has subsided considerably and will continue to do so as I am at last embracing and fully accepting my fairy self. The incredible experience I have just lived through has shown me that within that acceptance lies the knowing that one's true power is love and to radiate that love. Goodness, I have a lot to sift through and embody. I welcome the idea that my fairy self has the ability to transform lower vibrations to higher vibrations, and while here on my continuing earth walk, I can simply be a healing presence that supports others embarking on their own journeys of self-discovery."

Stella began to laugh before continuing "It's yet to be revealed what roads crossed or straight this acceptance will take me on."

She could still hear Crow's softly spoken words.

"Thank you, Stella, my fairy friend, I acknowledge that you have had an exciting and profound journey that has given you such amazing insights. I look forward to the time you are able and ready to share more. Make sure you now have your tea and rejoin us when you are ready. And Stella trust your Light Language."

Cassie brought her attention back to the sights and the sounds of their garden and before she went further down memory lane, she went in search of her phone to listen yet again to what she had recorded during the last session of the retreat. She remembered checking the time, which was strange in itself because she wasn't usually distracted by her phone during sessions. And had no recall of inadvertently pressing record. When she discovered what was on her phone with Stella's permission, she had listened to it numerous times. *Meant to be* she thought, as Stella's words helped to keep her on the track of living the concept of the fourth day.

Retrieving her phone from where it was charging, she resettled herself getting comfortable in her favourite chair. Once more in her mind's eye she pictured the final session. She'd noticed Stella slipping into the room and not being privy to the experience of others she had no way to gauge if they also felt the ripples of energy quietly emanating from Stella. Her attention returned to Crow's words as she was encouraging them all to continue with many of the processes learnt and practiced over the course of the weekend. Listening to others during the breaks she heard that some were focusing on only what resonated the most for them and what would be easily adaptable in their daily routines. Both her and Josh had already determined to follow through on most of the wisdom that Crow had imparted to each of them and use the simple processes they'd learnt for staying connected to the Angelic Realm.

As the afternoon drew to a close Crow invited feedback asking if anyone would like to share what knowledge or new understanding, each of us would take home. During a natural lull after many sharing's Stella began to speak in Light Language. Cassie always felt goosebumps when this memory resurfaced and remained grateful that her phone recorded these precious moments. Stella's voice was incredibly powerful and yet washed over them all gently in such a way that was reminiscent of the Singing Bowls played in last night's Sound Bath.

When the flow of words came to an end and after only taking a short pause Stella continued with the translation which Cassie and Josh listened to so many times.

"You are all part of the River of Light and Love. A current of energy which flows directly from the Creator.

Before your earth journey you planted seeds in that current of light. Seeds that have been scattered throughout the Universe in different dimensions throughout the Inner Planes.

Each of you holds the key to your own treasure chest. You are the key and when it is right timing and when you are awake enough, to your great delight you will discover the treasures you have stored that you can use to enrich your lives and remember your true natures.

Life can seem like a series of steppingstones to where you most wish to be. The steps may sometimes seem small and slow at different stages of your life then become great strides where you stretch yourself and Trust that Love is what connects you all to each other and to the Creator.

Use your abilities as the key wisely. Not only to use the gifts you left for yourself to discover but to unlock and embrace again your Innocence.

The Innocence that you were in your mother's womb remains intact as a pure, clear and unwritten upon divine canvas. It has never been tainted by the world's view that instigated the creation of doubts and fears that placed conditions on everything including Love. You only thought or were trained to believe it did.

Reconnecting with your Innocence unites you with the liquid light that flows through you and everyone."

She could still hear the silence as the flow and ebb of Stella's words came to an end. A silence that was charged with a swirling sacred energy which was then filled with the audible sounds of breaths being released. And she could still see the smiles which lit up everyone's faces.

Cassie was so deep into reliving these memories that it wasn't until she felt Josh's gentle hand on her shoulder that she realised that he had arrived home then saying with a smile.

"I am happy I made it home in time to listen in with you. It never fails to move me and remind me of what we have gained for ourselves and how the seeds we have planted for ourselves, and our relationship are flourishing."

"Aww Josh like Stella's your words give me goosebumps." then laughingly added "well baby and I are flourishing I am just happy I can still see my feet."

Drawing Cassie into a hug Josh whispered into her ear with a chuckle.

"I will keep an eye on them for you. But that reminds me I brought home some paint samples so we can decide on the colour for the nursery walls. If we arrive at a choice without lengthy deliberations, we might even get started on the painting."

"Josh I am choosing to ignore your dig at my past lengthy deliberations. I will try not to dither especially as we are in sync as I also bought some decals for the walls. We can see what works best with each sample. That's our weekend sorted. All things colour tomorrow then meeting both sets of parents for Sunday brunch."

By the impish glee on Josh's face, she knew that they were both recalling when they first met and in the getting to know you process it was soon revealed that their mothers shared the same first name. When they knew without a doubt that they were to be together and to save confusion Josh's mother being a few years older than her own claimed the right to be Therese. While hers was happy with the abbreviated Terri. If their baby was a girl, they knew including Therese in her name would please both their mums.

She decided there and then when their choices were made, she would send off some photos to Stella who was off on one of her and Barry's travels. They had set off in their new and impressive caravan and had only been gone for two weeks and were keeping in touch through photos and their accompanying stories. Sometimes it felt as though she was on the trip with them. As enjoyable as that was it was good knowing that they would be returning a couple of weeks before her due date.

Meister Eckhart

STELLA

New Ways

Stella and Barry were almost home from their close on two months long adventure, when she asked Barry to drop in to see Cassie and as it was the weekend, she thought they may get lucky, and find Josh home as well. But it would never do to just drop in, so she called them first and was delighted that Josh was indeed home and already putting the kettle on for a welcome home cup of tea.

After all Cassie's messages and photos of the nursery she couldn't wait to see the room in person then spend a small amount of time with Cassie and Josh before heading home to start unpacking. From their many conversations she knew that both Cassie and Josh were filled to the brim with excitement and anticipation as their baby's due date drew near. Their two would soon become three.

Cassie had been working from home the last few weeks and knowing Cassie's initial hesitancy, she felt happy for her that she had discovered that online consultations were as beneficial and fulfilling as face to face. This online success had reassured Cassie that when she was ready, she could continue to use this format to work with clients. And hold off on in person appointments until she and baby were in a good place. During one their phone conversations Cassie had mentioned that because the energetic connection wasn't missing, as she had once feared, she was quite liking the idea that in the future she could offer clients both methods for consultations.

Stella thought it a great idea as it would certainly allow her to reach out to those who lived further afield. Cassie, she knew used more than her technical and theoretical skills to tune into her clients' patterns of health to discover what was ailing them. Her ability to be fully present with her clients guaranteed that in the future many would continue to seek out her assistance.

After the exclamations and hugs of welcome home they put the cup of tea on hold and made their way to the nursery. Stella was so happy that Barry was with her and glancing at his face she knew they were caught up in a similar experience of being enfolded in the welcoming and loving embrace of the nursery Cassie and Josh had created. If Cassie and Josh knew their baby's sex, they weren't giving anything away. Neither of them had let anything slip.

The nursery was painted in the softer tones of colours found in nature, no indication of gender there. At first glance the large window could easily be mistaken for a magnificent painting. Until you noticed subtle perfumes wafting through the air bringing even more of the outside garden inside while the breeze created a gentle billowing of the sheer sage green curtains.

"Oh, Cassie and Josh, this is so beautiful. I know I can and am sure Barry will agree that we can feel the vibration of the love that you have poured into this room."

Nodding his head Barry began to put his thoughts into words.

"I agree with Stella and as I look around there is a sense of balance. The decals feature bright colours, yet they don't clash with the rest of the room." Both Barry and Stella's eyes were drawn to the highly polished timber cradle.

"Oh Josh." They both exclaimed at the same time as Barry continued "You have done such a wonderful job of restoring the cradle. Didn't this same cradle hold you and your brothers as babies?"

"Barry and I are definitely on the same page here. Josh, you have done a superb job. How precious that such a family treasure will hold the first grandchild for both sides of your families.

I am getting goosebumps seeing the bedding all ready and awaiting your bundle of joy."

Looking to Barry with a big smile she continued "I am so happy we dropped in, thanks Barry for supporting my suggestion. I am really glad you are here with me as I don't need to try to describe it to you. Whatever words I could conjure up wouldn't do this beautiful room, or the energy present, justice."

✦

When they finally arrived home, they had a bite to eat before cleaning and airing their van. They sorted what needed washing into piles to await tomorrow's washing marathon before turning their attention to opening all the windows of their house as an invitation to the gentle breeze to freshen all the long unoccupied rooms.

With things somewhat in hand and Barry happy to be back tinkering in his shed, she felt her garden calling her to do some tinkering herself. Fortunately, as arranged prior to their departure, their grass had been mown several times while they were on their travels, but some weeds and flowering shrubs in the need of trimming caught her eye.

She congratulated herself on having taken the trouble before they had set off to stock the pantry with nonperishable and everyday items and the freezer with premade meals. Adding to the fresh produce and refrigerated items they had purchased on their last stop meant that she wouldn't need to make a trip to the supermarket for a few days at least, maybe not even for a week.

There was nothing to prevent her from surrendering to the lure of her garden's call. What a wonderful way to spend the rest of the afternoon she thought. Being in the garden always seemed to put her in a reflective mood and she had discovered it to be the perfect place to review recent or past life events. Her experience in the Fairy Realm had wrought changes in how she saw and thought about herself. One thing she especially cherished was her new way of being able to maintain her attention, stay present and focus in the moment. Life when she stopped to notice was filled with many blessings to be grateful for. But sometimes she appreciated a review where she could marvel at how those new ways of thinking about herself, and life had arrived.

A story began playing out in her head and her first thoughts didn't go any further back than their recent travels and, reignited in that moment, the joy of how much Barry and herself loved exploring the out of way places that they discovered on their journey. Coupled with that was the joy of meeting interesting people along the way. And thinking back now she could see how effortless it seemed to be to find those that were open to discussing a wide range of topics. Many of these conversations whether short or long were often deep, meaningful and heartfelt. Leaving the energy of that connection made, long after they had parted ways.

In her mind's eye she could see the magnificence of the numerous clear nighttime skies they had witnessed. She had greeted the stars as if they were long lost friends and remembered when she'd gazed into them how blessed she felt that she didn't know all there was to know about the Universe, Galaxies and the Inner Planes. It was such a relief not to have to know everything at once. No longer needing to know everything negated any need to struggle or seek out what was next for her to learn. What she did learn on her magical journey was all she needed to be, was ready, and that required no anxious striving. It was as uncomplicated as being open to receive whatever wise information and insights she required to guide her daily. Each day, even those that had set plans in place, held the promise of continued adventures and the joy of new discoveries.

My she thought again, how she'd loved the magic of those clear night skies, they'd enhanced her awareness of what it meant to be conscious. For her It had become, whether she achieved it or not, as simple as consciously being present in the unfolding of each moment of her day, then living it. Without any sense of failure, some days she was better at doing so than others. *Yakazan*, she thought, would say her transformation was built on and would continue to be, on the seeds she had planted and the energy she had infused them with before incarnating. So much had been revealed to her during that time spent with Yakazan and she understood the progress towards this transformation was in her hands. Choosing to be transformation in action had resulted in her feeling somewhat bigger. Not in a physical sense but energetically. The word expanded fit comfortably with how she felt.

She was a lot calmer these days and because she watched them pass by without the need to struggle, this sense of expansion stayed with her wherever she went. She now thought back to when this clear understanding had taken root. One, that had enabled her to embody the truth in the Liquid Light Woman's words that she didn't need to do anything to be a healing presence for others. Travelling had also added another layer to this understanding. When travelling she wasn't anyone's mother, sister, friend or therapist. She was simply being herself. And wonders of wonders the people she met seemed to enjoy being in her presence. It struck her that their time away had a retreat like quality about it as it had also been filled with meaningful insights.

She now looked forward to walking through her days trusting that she would be guided to the truths, people and situations that would resonate with her. And whatever information she needed to know or an action that was required in any given moment would turn up. This added a freshness and sparkle to each day. Yes, she considered for a moment, the road ahead may not always be smooth, but nothing could prevent her constant forward motion and transformation unless she allowed it. It was on her if she stifled or put limits on her progress.

Another thought floating through her mind beckoned her to make a similar vow here in her own garden that she had made towards the end of Crow's retreat. She'd made a promise to herself after the magical events that had occurred to never again write off her insights as just her imagination.

Her recall of hers and Barry's time away kept circling back to the impact of those clear nighttime skies. They had had aided her in her quest to transcend the dense energy of earth and energetically tune into the colours and vibrations found throughout the Universe. During her meditation practices under the stars, shafts of light splashed through her and that light filled her with the sensation of being transported to the peak of a high mountain where she could sit and reach out and to connect with the stars and other galaxies. And was aware that from that peak, she could travel to other dimensions and just as the Liquid Light woman had predicted, make connections with other aspects of herself. If she was a computer she could use the terms, downloads and updates to describe the pure energy and joy that she experienced and brought back to her physical body at the end of these blissful meditations.

It amused her that when to she relived her mediative experience or thought about describing it to others how terms associated with computer technology had taken up residence in her words. This new vocabulary surprised her because she remembered telling Cassie and Josh how often she grappled with understanding technology and its continued advances and updates. But she knew how to ask for help when needed and never felt less than for asking. One of her grandson's loved to remind her that for her generation the advent of computers was akin to being in a foreign country and not able to speak the language.

No vocabulary she thought or artificial intelligence could duplicate the ability for herself and others to hold and radiate higher vibrations of Light.

My goodness her thoughts had wandered far away from seeing in her mind the areas and scenic trails they had chosen to explore. They had both delighted in the sheer pleasure and restorative quality of being surrounded by the beauty of nature. She gave Barry full credit for never disbelieving her or rolling his eyes when she had recounted her adventures in the Fairy realm or when she shared that the physical activity of walking in nature while being focused on gratitude had also become a spiritual practice for her. A practice that always reminded her that she was so much more than her human self, and likewise there was more beyond what the physical eyes could see.

She smiled to herself enjoying the memory of how Barry had become used to her stopping to whisper thank you to all her eyes alighted on. He was even stopping and adding his own thanks when they paused to admire a tree, a shrub, a flower, a body of water, a hillside, a meadow, birds in flight across a blue sky, intriguing cloud formations or whatever vista filled them with calm delight. Barry had even become used to her having conversations with any part of nature that drew her attention. She had previously shared with Barry that if one listened closely enough, nature had a story to share and used the lemon tree, she had stumbled across, some time ago, in a field of rolling grass to illustrate the origins of this idea.

She had fully described to him her adventure of coming across the small lemon tree that was almost hidden under long grass roots and yet was producing fruit that was surrounded by shiny green leaves. When she had stopped to admire the small but healthy tree, she had been surprised by what it had to say. Words she would never forget.

"Thank you for connecting with me. And though I am somewhat obscured by what is around me nothing can change the fact that I am a lemon tree. I nourish myself with the nutrients found within the soil and know that my seed-bearing fruit can be of service in many ways. When my fruit is picked to share, I continue to generate more."

In the retelling she mentioned that her focus on the lemon tree had been so intense that she hadn't noticed the silence. And only when her astonishment subsided, she had gradually become aware of the returning sounds of nature. And that at first, they were somewhat hushed before filling the air with the songs and calls of the birds, the sound of the breeze in the treetops and the buzz of known and unknown insects. And because Barry knew about Yakazan she could share every time she revisited this special moment, the taste of the delight she experienced on hearing and remembering the words Yakazan whispered in her ear.

"Stella explore the imagery and guidance of the Lemon Tree's wise words they can be easily applied to Human life. Nature has beautiful surprises that can enhance lives rather than detract from it. Keep looking and listening."

Then after the briefest of pauses more of Yakazan's clear and simple words flooded her mind.

> *"There is no pretense in Nature. A raindrop is a raindrop.*
> *A lemon a lemon. A bird a bird. And each bird's song their own*
> *and yet connected in harmony with no need to compete.*
> *Each call is heard and honoured."*

Stella welcomed the tingling sensations that these memories triggered and took some more time to enjoy them and savour Barry's acceptance of her words. Her memories of clear night skies, meditations and experiences in nature were slowly fading and as the images dropped away returning her to the present moment, her gaze, took in and was drawn to the sky, noticing the changes to the cloud formations that indicated that sunset wasn't imminent but was on its way. Her mother would have said she was 'wool gathering.' Which was a phrase her mother said was an apt description that applied to her when she was growing up.

Looking from the sky back to her garden she was rather bemused to notice how productive her 'wool gathering' had been when she noticed the mounds of clippings and weeds ready to go in the compost bin. She smiled and despite what her mother may had said about being lost in thoughts she enjoyed the delicious physical side effects and lightheartedness her reminiscing had created and would carry that into the remaining chores of this day. Like the Dwarfs she was more than happy to whistle while she worked. Though singing was more her style.

She felt blessed and grateful to have had the amazing experiences that inspired these memories and their effects. And right now, she was also glad to be home and ready for what tomorrow, a new day would bring.

A New Day

Today was a new day and the images and the wonderful memories from their holiday were now in residence in what she often referred to as the filing cabinets in her mind. The evening before they couldn't decide whether to be overwhelmed or impressed by the sheer abundance of photos taken on their trip. And had begun the sorting process of what to download and copy as physical reminders. There were many that were worthy of being framed and found themselves sending some to their iCloud storage, confident that they would remember how to retrieve them. There she thought to herself, look, how easily that technical lingo slipped through her mind.

Both her and Barry had become used to being up and about to greet each new day's arrival and this morning was no exception and had her setting out early on her morning walk.

She couldn't deny how happy she was to be home and able to head off to one of her favourite walking routes. It was when she set out, she realised that walkers were indeed a small community within the larger community and that her nonappearance had been noticed. She cheerfully acknowledged and returned the waves and uttered good mornings of so many familiar faces while also enjoying "welcome backs "and the "good to see you," comments being sent her way. In the past she often joked to them that her shorter strides meant that she walked twice as far as those with longer legs.

Those shorter yet fast strides were now taking her in the direction of the bush tracks she enjoyed where once you left the signs of suburbia behind it felt like you were entering a hidden forest. Just as she set her feet in this direction, she met up with Kathy a sometimes-walking buddy exiting the area. First names she usually remembered and had them listed in her phone contacts under the surname 'Walking.' Made it easier to arrange a walk that also included a coffee stop.

Kathy's face was beaming when she caught site of her.

"OH, Stella great to see you back I would keep walking with you but need to get home. Text me and let's see when we can fit in a walk, chat and coffee time."

"Will do Kathy, and it's good to see you looking so well now. I will be in touch soon."

Then before heading off Kathy turned back with a bemused look on her face. "Stella your shoes are still the whitest of whites. Are they another new pair? How do you keep them so clean? One day I hope you will tell me what product you use."

"Ahh dear Kathy, no they're not new. What keeps them clean? Fairy magic of course!" She exclaimed then laughed when Kathy's words floated back to her "Sure, Stella, magic. The name of the product will do."

Laughing Stella wondered what Kathy's reaction would be if she told her that the brightness of her shoes responded to her own vibrations. Rather like how a barometer is influenced by atmospheric changes. On the return from an overseas trip just over a year ago, her shoes were as dull as she felt. Jet lag had knocked her flat, more so than usual. As her energy picked up and she had slowly returned to the higher vibrations of her normal optimistic self. Her shoes increased in brightness. In contrast to that occasion on arrival home from this most recent trip, she felt well rested and relaxed. Restored was the word she could use to describe her present state. Yet when they had set out that hadn't felt like what she had needed. As she continued on her walk the word in alignment popped into her mind. Yes, that described it perfectly she thought. Their journey had taken them through majestic national parks along dramatic coastlines. Through relaxing countryside. And their lengthy stays at each location allowed her to absorb and connect with every different landscape making it possible to follow through with her one of her intentions to align her soul and fairy nature with the spirit of the nature beings of the earth, the trees, the air and the water. The brightness of her shoes matched the raising of her own vibrations. Even when walking along rain affected tracks. She could only agree with her own statement that it's "fairy magic "at work.

In reality what she thought of as a hidden forest was an area filled with pathways winding through the trees and native shrubs with some wooden bridges skirting the many creeks that all fed into the close by lake. What may have once been called swamp was now known by today's popular name, wetlands. Whatever name was given to this area it was such a pleasure to be greeted by the sight of wildflowers in bloom and the plentiful ferns among the trees.

Coming to a fork in the track she quickly decided to continue walking along the creek in a direction that would take her away from the lake knowing there was a wooden bench some distance along where she could sit awhile before retracing her steps and head back towards the lake. This was a good time of day to check out the birdlife that flitted through the trees then move on to watching the ibis and egrets that favoured the marshy shallows created where the creeks and lake met. She hoped the black swans would be there. The pair that often glided in this area reminded her of Cassie and Josh and even of Barry and herself. They might peck at each other now and then but continued to glide side by side supporting one another.

For now, though as she sat her eyes were drawn to the reflection of the sky and trees in the creek. And as always thought of how much sharper and clearer reflections appeared by comparison to what was being reflected. The sky seemed bluer the trees more alive which all added to the wonder of everything her eyes noticed.

That's it, she thought coming up with an acronym for the word new. She loved acronyms and this one must be just right as it slid so easily into her mind. Notice Each Wonder and that is exactly what she was doing right now and what she had been doing while away. Being present and noticing each wonder described perfectly the connection she was able to make with everything within her and her surroundings.

These joyous thoughts led her to deciding from the moment of waking to apply it to the start of each new day and to how use this approach began to unfold in her mind. Firstly, greet the morning, then begin deep breathing and notice the sensations created by those deep breaths as a prelude to settling into a deep meditative state. Then allow for the wonder of achieving a blissful state of stillness even if only for a few moments. To then embrace the opportunity to choose love with the intention that it would flow through the day ahead regardless of the challenges. And when they arose to not withhold love from herself or any situation where judgement could so easily step in instead.

To notice when unhappy, and when cringe worthy memories could unexpectedly surface. And rather than judge herself, celebrate the wonder that she noticed that she wasn't being who she wished to be in those moments. She was liking where her thoughts were taking her and was more than ready to commit to starting each new day trusting that the power of Love was always present. Then rather than being triggered into a reaction she could get creative instead. Acknowledging that in catching and noticing the effects of these triggers she could release and dissolve them and send them on their way with love.

Feeling content with the direction of her thoughts she remembered how she favoured the French word for love, Amor and enjoyed using it. As it rolled off her tongue it sounded like 'ah more' she would always instantly think of it as love creating more love. Sighing deeply as she focused on Amor, she grew excited as she marveled at the perfect partnership her new day and new ways were forming. In that moment she easily recaptured her experience of flying. Was that a flutter of wings she could feel?

Glancing at her shoes she noted that they were glowing *they must agree with where my thoughts are taking me,* she smiled to herself. Not only were they glowing but also felt supercharged as they nudged her to get up and get moving again. It seemed no time at all as she made her way back to the fork in the track before heading towards the lake only coming to a stop when she made her way to the lake's edge. She began practicing noticing each wonder and was delighted to see the ibis and egrets then felt blessed and excited to not only see the black swans but a trio of offspring following in their wake.

Her attention was drawn away from the swans to the buzzing of a text in the back pocket of her jeans. Reading it filled her with excitement and anticipation and with one final glance at the swans she set out to make her way home at a brisk pace to share Josh's group text with Barry.

"Hi all," it read "I am letting you all know we are on our way to the birthing Centre. It doesn't seem as though baby wants to wait for another two weeks. It will probably be a while yet, but her midwife said to bring her in. Will be in touch when I can. Love to you all."

CASSIE

Their Precious Gem

A gentle mid-morning breeze moved the curtains of the nursery as she sat gazing into the eyes of her and Josh's bundle of joy. At three months old she was already bright, and alert and she was sure she could see a store house of wisdom in her eyes. Stella Therese was a real gem and in the language of her grandmothers, a perfect baby.

The memory of Stella's reaction to hearing that their first born carried her name would always stay with her. Together on speaker phone they had firstly let her, and Barry know that their daughter had arrived safely before going on to tell them her name. Through the phone they could hear Stella's tears of joy as Josh shared with her that for them, she lived up to her name and was a bright shining star that had helped them find their way back to one another. She smiled as she remembered that for once Stella had been so overwhelmed that she was speechless. Not the usual gregarious Stella they were used to.

Gurgles, chuckles and smiles were becoming a regular feature during baby Stella's waking hours. Crying only to call attention to her needs especially if something wasn't to her liking. Josh was such a loving and competent dad. Cassie never failed to express her gratitude to him for feeding Stella at the witching hour. And assured of her father's love she always settled quickly. Neither of them were naive enough to think there wouldn't be some future unsettled times but after surviving those sleep deprived early few weeks, they knew they made a good team supporting one another.

Looking out into the garden always calmed her and seemed to have the same effect on Stella Therese. Casting her glance around the room her eyes settled on the framed poem that Josh had written in calligraphy on embossed paper. He had written it not long after their retreat. 'I am an architect 'he kept saying 'not a poet 'but had gone on to share with her how he could no longer ignore the words that kept making their presence felt until he finally put pen to paper. It was important for Josh to display them as a reminder that they both contributed to their relationship. To trust that even with sometimes differing ideas they could still work together. To move past thinking that he had to have all the answers about what was best for both of them. And to Trust that who they were individually and together was supported by an unseen force beyond them. He had also shared with her that the words resonated with what he had come to understand about the Creator 's vibrations of Light and Love that filled every part of the Universe.

After dithering about where to hang it they finally agreed that the nursery was the perfect place to mount this much read poem. The nursery had indeed become the most go to room in their house. As she began to read the words again it crossed her mind that the times, they were on the same wavelength were such a gift.

I was a star.
Shining, brilliant
High, aloft
But as is the fate.
Of stars
Like hope falling and
Dashed from the skies.
Such puffed up loftiness.
Dissolved.
Until I finally realised
I don't shine alone.
This brilliance is not only of me.
And we are taken to the heights.
Held aloft,

Supported by a power.

Not of me but we.

And as I remember.

This power that supports us

My heart opens and opens to Love.

And once again

From the heights

Yet also from the depths

Together with Clarity

We Beam.

She thought for a moment about their frequent and lengthy discussions about their roles as parents. Discussions that led to what they would like to pass onto baby Stella and any children they may be blessed with in the future or as they liked to say, more gems. Josh and herself were determined that they would know that they were loved and that their love didn't need to be earned. That they would always be enough and there was no competition they needed to win or lose to be loved and didn't need to always get something right or try to be better than anyone else. They were only in the early stages of parenting and were sure they had much to learn along the way but hoped their ideas would find their way into action, and not be forgotten, when and if such situations arose. For now, they were content having their delightful little person as the recipient of their love.

She knew that how they envisioned themselves as parents also applied to their relationship with each other. In the quiet of the nursery, she could imagine Stella sitting next to her saying the words she'd often heard her share.

"How I envy your generation knowing these truths now. You didn't have to wait until you were fifty or older to gain such wisdom. And now so many of this new generation will also carry this knowledge. There's such hope that love will spread faster than the fear of previous generations."

Stella's vision for Mother Earth aligned with both her own and

Josh's. At first being new parents had seemed overwhelming. How could the choices they were making in regard to their relationship and the family life they wished to create help create a better world? How could their efforts contribute to the whole?

Each question they asked and with each doubt, because they were realistic enough to know there could be challenging times ahead, they came back to the poem especially reciting the line "This power that supports us."

Together they had decided that by simply being themselves and starting in small ways with baby steps was better than not taking any steps. Baby steps had the potential to grow into bigger steps. It was hard to deny what was happening on Mother Earth but the love and the joy they brought to being parents which they hoped would be the hallmark of their family life was a great place to start.

She gently placed their now sleeping soundly, precious gem, into her crib and watched as a smile seemed to flit across her sleeping daughter's face. And like so many times before wondered if she felt an energetic connection to all the previous infants, including her father, who had thrived in this beautifully crafted cradle.

Time to get on with some chores before the next feed, she thought, only to find her thoughts veering back to their dear friend and confidant Stella. She often mused that one of the most fascinating things about Stella was that you never felt judged regardless of what you shared with her. She never tried to impart her ideas or gave any obvious advice. There was something magical about being in her presence that seemed to inspire and open your own mind to the best or possible solutions. Just being in her company seemed to unlock something in her own mindset.

The beauty of that was that Stella seemed blissfully unaware of this superpower of hers to simply inspire. She wasn't trying to be held in high regard or be perceived as special she genuinely cared and loved all those she came into contact with. It worked.

Meister Eckhart

 # STELLA 

Joy in
The Afternoon

Stella arrived home from grocery shopping in high spirits and was delighted to be able to recount to Barry that her pre shopping visit to see Cassie and her namesake had found them both well with baby Stella awake and gurgling away. In today's world even the faces of newly born babies appeared wise, and it often seemed as though they were ready to settle in and have a lengthy conversation. And of course, she was only too happy to oblige with baby Stella and also enjoyed walking around and sitting with her in the beautiful garden that Cassie and Josh had created.

Groceries put away and lunch over she became lost in her thoughts as she remembered how often she'd heard her friends express the same sentiment about the wise souls visible in the new generation of lights arriving on Mother earth. Her firstborn son had arrived while she was in her late teens and by the time, she was in her mid-twenties, his two brothers had joined him. She had done her best to be a good mother but looking back she realised that she had a lot of growing up to do herself. She had certainly needed those seeds of hers. Perhaps one of the reasons for newly arrived babies appearing so wise, was that many parents were well into their twenties or older when they welcomed their much-loved little ones. They were parents that had time to mature mentally and spiritually through their life's experience.

That certainly rang true for Cassie and Josh, she thought. Just by being themselves, they were reflecting their wisdom to baby Stella. Of course, new parents of Cassie and Josh's generation and the new generation they were creating would have their own crossroads or pivotal changes to contend with, but there was such hope in her own heart that the power of love would become and remain entrenched within them. They carried her dream of how life could be on Mother Earth. Trusting that wisdom would guide them to know when to sidestep any stress attached to crossroads or changes and know what direction to take.

Such thoughts didn't weigh her down but filled her with joy and with a cup of tea in hand she wandered into her garden. Making her way to sit on a wooden bench in the dappled shade of one of the many trees that stood proudly in their yard. Trees which personified the qualities of strength and courage. She could see flashes of lorikeets and parrots amongst the many branches, hear their calls and the whispers of the leaves created by a gentle breeze and yes by the fairies in their garden. She was always captivated by the music found in nature.

Her own personal and emotional crossroads had led her on a magical journey. One that had expanded her fields of awareness. There had been no weakening in her intentions to continue moving forward embracing more love and light. In fact, her sense of purpose had strengthened. This purpose and resolve had replaced her previous sense of lostness. She was often bemused by the fact, that when thoughts of self judgement and doubt sometimes turned up, her confidence never once wavered, that the seeds she planted were aligned with her truth and that they would continue to grow and blossom.

Sitting quietly under the trees she gently chastised herself for forgetting to pass on to Barry the greetings from the friends she had met and talked to briefly while shopping. And of course, they asked their usual question.

"Stella how you are enjoying retirement? We loved seeing your photos on Facebook and reading about your travels."

How easily that retirement word seemed to roll off their tongues. But it was a word that did weigh heavily on her and one she really didn't like. I *need to come up with another word* she thought.

Meanwhile regardless of the word she used to describe this stage of her life she had found it difficult at first to live days without the structure she was used to. By her own design her time had been structured into a routine of workdays with scheduled client appointments. She did balance that with a day off in order to do the paperwork side of her business. That structure had worked well for her. She knew what was required and when, but it didn't always allow for spontaneity. Some schedules could be changed but not often. In those early days of her so named retirement, she found she was busy, though if pressed to explain what was keeping her busy, specifics often eluded her, and she wasn't quite sure what exactly was keeping her so busy. Perhaps 'I'm busy', had become an automatic response in today's world.

When discussing this with her sister-in-law Johanna, her words rang true and made sense.

"You suddenly have all this time to fill, and you fill it up by being busy."

The silver lining, she eventually discovered and had grown to appreciate was that she had time for spontaneity and socialising. And was able to set off without any qualms on her travels with Barry. She had lost that sense that she was running out of time, and valued being able to take moments like this, when she could sit quietly. In this present period of quietness, she was delighted when the word refocus just gently slipped into her thoughts. *Refocusing*, she thought was the word she would use from now on to describe the art of creating changes in her life. Yes, it was another R word, but she welcomed it into her thoughts. It sat well with her and was much more to her liking than the word retirement. And it beautifully described her progress from feeling adrift to creating a more user-friendly structure in her life.

The simple change of a word lifted her spirits in such a way that she also felt physically lighter. And matched how lighter her earth walk had become without any need to strive or try to make such a sense of lightness happen. Daily she rejoiced that her time with Yakazan in the fairy realm had reintroduced her to her seeds of Courage, Willingness and Trust. The connection to both Yakazan and her seeds remained strong and constant. Sometimes she remained oblivious to that connection, *after all she was still human,* she thought. When she was aware of that connection, she found she was able to keep walking in her human form with a bounce in her step. And didn't question when noticing the occasional flutter of her invisible wings. The trees around her seemed to sigh with relief that she had become so accepting of her wings and had stopped dismissing them as her imagination.

Hearing her own deep sigh of contentment confirmed how happy she was with what her refocusing had achieved. She had indeed found a way to refocus and recreate her life to be more balanced with a fluid structure that was more suited to her days and current needs. After floundering on the surface filling up her days with busyness, she had reset her priorities on what added meaning to each day. The joy she found in guiding and helping others was satisfied by scheduling regular and well attended mentoring days for therapists.

The words of both Yakazan and the Liquid Light Woman about simply being a healing presence remained in the forefront of her mind. The mentoring days and other discussion groups she facilitated gave her the opportunity to simply be this healing presence.

In this way, even if it was only in her small pocket of the universe, along with the fairies in the woods, forest and gardens, she was contributing to raising vibrations, her own and Mother Earth's.

Stella couldn't help but smile when at the same time she thought *love is the gift that keeps on giving* popped into her mind she looked up and saw Barry carrying a tray with mugs and some sweet treats making his way towards her. Barry had certainly come to love cooking. Never in her wildest dreams would she had thought it would be so. But it had come to pass after Barry had gone to healthy gourmet cooking classes, fulfilling a long-held dream that he had kept to himself. She cherished the fact that they could still surprise one another and from the joy on his face it was obvious how much pleasure he derived from this newfound creative outlet. She was certainly a grateful recipient of his culinary skills.

"Hi Hun, I thought I would join you and have come bearing gifts, your favourite herbal blend and some choc chip slice."

Moving along the bench Stella was only too happy to make room for Barry as he placed the tray gently between them.

"Aww, thanks Barry all this fresh air has me feeling peckish and ready for another cup of tea. You spoil me so. I love this slice and I love watching how happy you are in the kitchen. You put so much thought into what you prepare."

"Stella I am just happy that you appreciate everything I dish up. You know I still enjoy keeping the yard up to scratch and planning trips away. That gives me an idea I might just start working on some picnic menus and plan some day trips. There's plenty of delightful beaches and national parks that aren't too far away. I will put some thought into it and then check which days work best for you. Back to what I was going to say, when I am preparing food and especially when I am devising my own recipes. I visualise how the ingredients blend together and can sense how their combination will taste. I am not painting a masterpiece or like you putting words together that result in a poem, and yet I feel like an artist creating meals and treats that look and taste great. I like to think I have found a space of love where I can be love and create from love."

"Yes, Barry you have always been such a wonderful organiser and that also takes a lot of creative effort but in the kitchen your true artistry shines through. And not only can I see it Barry, but the organisers of the charity cake stall you contributed to were also amazed by your contributions. I heard the word 'artform' mentioned several times, but I wonder if they realise that your secret ingredient is love. I can taste it."

"Thanks Hun, I adore you for noticing, and using the word shine because that's how it feels. You may not realise this but often I watch you while you are meditating. You are so still, and I see you there but wonder where you are. Here or somewhere on the inner planes I hear you and Cassie talk about, or in what dimension. Are you talking to the Liquid Light Woman? And silly a thought I know but will you get lost, are you ok? But then I drink in the luminous glow of your face but as I think of it now your whole presence seems to glow. You also carry that glow throughout the day, and I revel in the fact that I have found that cooking is my form of meditation. Yes, an active one, I know, but one that adds a bit of shine to how I think about myself."

As Barry shared what he was experiencing Stella was deeply moved by the passion she could see in his eyes. *Creating and living our lives as works of art, turned up wearing many faces* she thought. Healing was an art and listening was an art. She was sure she could think of so many more but in that moment, she just wished to get up and give Barry a big hug. Sitting, Barry was just the right height for her to give him a heart-to-heart hug which he enthusiastically returned.

"That was a delicious hug, Barry. I am so happy that you have found something that you are so passionate about. And I hope I say thank you enough, so you understand how grateful I am not only for the feasts you prepare but for how supportive and encouraging you have been during our years together. We perceive the world from different viewpoints, and it has never been a wedge between us but a bridge we can cross to understanding each other. Sometimes that can be challenging yet liberating at the same time. And it works both ways, you never expect me to think or be like you and I have no need for you to think or be like me. But please do set aside any concerns that I will get lost."

"Stella thank goodness you are not like me as I know in the past an apt description of myself would definitely be that of a cantankerous grump. With the pleasure and joy, I am finding in cooking I am hoping to change that description to a joyful grump."

Barry's self analysis had them both laughing.

"I think that you deserve another hug, Barry. Another heart to heart one."

After the hug she moved the tray in order to sit next to Barry and snuggle against him to prolong this delightful moment of connection. She was grateful for her experience in the fairy realm and across other dimensions, but she understood that in order to anchor wisdom and knowledge on the earth plane she needed to interact energetically and physically in this reality. And moments like this with Barry and when she connected with others made life on this Earth fulfilling and meaningful.

"Guess what Barry?" Stella said while releasing a big sigh. "I think we have each found our own way to be of service in this world of ours. I don't think we can ever have too much joy to share in whatever manner we can. Like a smile joy is contagious and if enough catch it, think of how far it can spread. I like to think everywhere. Barry you are such a charming human, being happy and then doing something that you enjoy."

Barry's quick response, "And Stella you have such a way with words." Had them both dissolving into laughter. It took more than a few moments before he could continue.

"Do you remember that television commercial from years ago Stella, where the voice over says, 'wait there's more!'? Your words brought that phrase to mind. I agree there can never be too much joy. I am on board with that. Right now, as it's my turn to cook dinner I better get on with that. But before I do, and as we have been having this heart to heart, and just in case I don't say it enough, I am so grateful you are in my life. Many of your friends describe you as a 'pocket rocket' which is so accurate. You may not think it does but your joy and the delight that you find even in the smallest of things inspires me to lighten up and cease seeing everything in the world as a heavy load on my own shoulders. I admire the way you interact with others and support them to seek out and find their own life paths to walk. And I don't know how you do it, but you never judge or even suggest what their truth is or could be. Wow Stella I am so lucky to get to live with a 'pocket rocket.'"

As if a button had been pushed tears filled and flowed from Stella's eyes which she sought to quickly explain" Barry these are tears of joy. Thank you. My goodness this has been a special afternoon. I know we have had many deep conversations before, but I have the sense that we are both on the same page to start spreading more joy. Can't wait to eat this evening's love meal. But please another hug before you go."

Life as a Book

Stella watched as Barry made his way back to the house sensing the moment that he would turn around to catch her smile. As a man of many talents, he was able to balance the tray, put his fingers to his lips and throw her a kiss which she in turn captured and placed in her heart. This habit of theirs could always be depended upon to produce more smiles and laughter.

As he turned to be on his way again, she marveled at the new chapters Barry was adding to his life's story. His latest chapters were filled with such joy that they seemed to have a spillover effect on their surroundings. Flowers and shrubs were even blooming in areas shaded by the many trees in their back and front yard. The bird population appeared to have increased which gave their blended calls and songs, choir status, and somehow the trees seemed healthier, sturdier and leaves greener. Except for the fact that visitors had made similar comments she might have labelled her thinking as fanciful.

She turned her thoughts to the chapters she had added to her own story with all its endings that had become new beginnings. When Barry was finally out of sight, she fell into contemplating that if her life was a book and knowing that books had a beginning, middle and an end and possibly an epilogue, what part of the book had she reached? Past the middle and with fingers mentally crossed she hoped nowhere near the end.

Her thoughts were then off and running. She could acknowledge that at different stages of her life a number of characters played a role in her story for a short time before returning to their own. While others had a lengthier stay. Her and Barry were a part of one another's stories maintaining their connection in chapters shared and read and yet also had their own. She was enjoying her ponderings but wasn't too preoccupied by where they were taking her that she didn't notice a slight energetic shift next to her which was accompanied by Yakazan's shimmering presence. A presence which she welcomed with joy. These unplanned yet welcome appearances were becoming more frequent and were always as exciting as they were helpful.

"How delightful Yakazan, I really love it when you simply pop in! Your insights never fail to inspire me."

"I love surprising you Stella with a shimmer or two and because we maintain our connection, I can gladly inform you that you are nowhere near finishing this earthly walk. You definitely have more wisdom and joy to share. There are many who trust you. When you quietly share ideas about living with a sense of expanded awareness, that goes beyond usual human perception, you are listened to."

As always Yakazan's gentle words brought a smile to her face." Phew, thank you for confirming that I have more chapters to come. Even if I had doubts, I do try to maintain various amounts of focus on my seeds knowing that they will help the way ahead remain clear."

"Stella, if you were to narrate your life book up until now, would it be divided into sections? If so, how would you describe them?"

Yakazan's question kept her quiet for a couple of minutes before she found an answer that sat well with her. "That's an interesting question you have sprung on me, Yakazan, and one I will answer from my human perspective. What first comes to mind is Part One, Two and Three. That seems like a reasonable description even if it lacks imagination. I feel a bit more inventive giving each section a title and it fits well with part one to be called 'While Asleep'.

I have no desire to return to those early years from cradle to adolescence and moving into early adulthood. Yes, there were bright moments scattered throughout but I can take myself back there in my thoughts and still feel the sense of the sleepwalking and the forgetfulness that prevailed during those years."

More shimmering was happening next to her, and she took that to be Yakazan's nod of agreement." Stella that is a good description and a necessary one, which I know you now understand. Except for moments of magical sharp clarity, the mists or veils of forgetfulness led you to live out of the creations of your human mind. Some of those worked out and some didn't. But it was what you had chosen to explore and experience. Think I can work out what you would name Part Two."

Laughing Stella continued," yes it can only be called 'Waking Up.' A maturing time. Looking back, I can clearly recall that it was sometimes extremely painful evolving beyond the human condition and awakening to regarding myself as a spiritual being and a Fairy at that. Too much tumultuous water has passed under the bridge for me to even wish for the obliviousness of sleep. My desire to awaken surpasses any desire I might have to do so.

And jumping into Part Three I don't think I could call it anything but the 'Ongoing Now.' I am optimistic that an ever-growing inner wisdom may continue to fill Part three. Replacing any of the dramas and angst of my earlier chapters with perpetual cycles of embracing, embodying and acceptance. When doubts and fears turn up and make their presence felt during the challenges of my daily life, I never fail to value, be grateful for, and use those seeds I planted."

She sensed more shimmer like agreement before Yakazan asked her, "What title would you give to your life book Stella?"

It didn't take much effort to ponder as she quickly replied," I would call it 'Head in the Clouds and Feet on the Ground.' "

"A good description Stella. Though another good title could be 'Practical Spirituality.' It's also worth considering because I have heard you say to yourself when your mind has been bursting with ideas and knowledge new to you that if whatever understanding and insights you have gained can't be applied to your daily living what are their earthly use".

"Mm Yakazan, yes, another good title but I do enjoy having my head in the clouds. I am happy to be able say that in both my previous and current pages and chapters I am able to step back to review my experiences in Part One and Two and now in Part Three as all occurring in Divine timing. May not have appeared to have been Divine intervention at the time but I can now accept that all of my experiences were lived events that guided me to this point in time. Looking ahead though I would like my new chapters to be filled with joyful experiences rather than just words about joy. In this world Joy can sometimes be a word that others find annoying or hard to swallow when they're wholly focused only on the calamities that occur almost daily on this planet."

"Well Stella, I think I know what words annoy you. When you first started to wake up you really didn't like the term 'let it go' and now I sense your reaction when you hear that phrase 'you've got this.'"

"I know I do. Intellectually, I understand the meaning behind the phrases but in those early days of waking up, being told by well-meaning others to 'let it go' often felt confusing. Sometimes it seemed like plain hard work to find what I had to let go of and where to. I know that may seem like a silly thought but at the time I also felt judged. Then there were times when I shared some feelings that were meaningful for me, and rather than have them acknowledged, was told to let them go. When that happened, it was as if a stone filled with hurt would lodge in my stomach. If this hadn't been my waking up stage, it would have been so easy to slip into a pit of despair and remain stuck there. Instead, during this time period becoming more conscious of the cause and effects of my thoughts and behaviors, allowed me to gradually view and explore these effects as an opportunity to make different and more supportive life choices. There are still times when life can feel like hard work, but fortunately my awareness about the power of choice keeps growing."

With her thoughts back in that part of her life she noticed that she was holding her neck bent to one side. It was getting stiff, and she promptly brought it back to its natural midline position. Repositioning her head also brought her focus from past thoughts back to the present.

"Again, looking back to that stage, I placed two words 'I release….'" before whatever I needed to send on its way. It became my phrase of choice and I continue to use it. It struck me as being a gentler word, and I discovered operating this way provided me with many lightbulb moments. I continue to use this phrase and always enjoy the clarity those lightbulb moments bring with them. I have also added the phrase 'stop it' to my internal dialogue."

"A good phrase." she heard Yakazan say before adding" Think, for a moment what do a lot of humans, you included Stella most need to 'stop' doing? What makes moving forward difficult.?"

"That doesn't need much thinking about Yakazan. Pretty sure you mean stop self-judgment. From my own experience it's one of the fastest ways to bring me to a full stop. My goodness there are so many things to stop doing. Trying to control outcomes and staying attached to unsupportive past events being among them. 'I release all known and unknown negative thoughts I hold about myself', works well for me during such times."

Stella sensed Yakazan waiting for her to continue this discussion about words and the birds were even hushed for a moment while she got her thoughts in order hoping what she had to say would make sense because she knew how many people used the other phrase that bugged her.

"Let me see if I can explain the what and the why because I never wish to judge or belittle others that use it. Here goes, it's the phrase you mentioned 'You've got this.' When I hear it or it's been said to me, my quirky sense of humour kicks in as I think which 'this' have I got or going to get. I translate 'got this' into 'I can.' For example, 'I can allow my intuition to guide me 'or 'I can look into this situation and see what I need to heal within me.' I have also grown to enjoy the phrases 'just being' or 'just is.' In my own mind when I am in either state, I don't need to let go or be gotten as I experience my spirit mind creating calm and balance. My inner and outer worlds seem to right themselves and my human life becomes bearable once more."

"And how would you like that human experience to be?"

"That's a big question, Yakazan. My human mind can get all anxious and walk a path caught up with fears and concerns. While my Spirit mind if I let it and tune into it, steers me onto a path of joy where doubts and fears can be met and dissolved with love. Talking about Spirit mind fuels my desire to just know 'I am love' and to live from that space. No more searching for it. Simply be it. But then the human mind seems to like complications rather than simplicity. Us humans even when we know there's more to us than we ever thought can be a funny lot."

It seemed to Stella that Yakazan's shimmer became even brighter.

"Stella excuse the pun; I got your explanations. Words and phrases carry so much energy with them. They can paint pictures of both light and shade as well as create balance. And like the seeds you planted they can seed 'a gem of an idea.' Stella, keep using the words and phrases that make sense to you. And how you experience life."

Stella couldn't help but laugh and agree with Yakazan." Thank you and luckily some of those gems get past the idea stage! And perhaps I owe that to planting the correct seeds for me."

"So true Stella and being with you as you discovered those seeds was as much a memorable adventure for me as it was for you. I have mentioned before that our time together took you to where you left them, in place, waiting, they were never buried. You only needed to open your internal eyes to acknowledge them. Each human may think they need to search for the treasures buried within and seem to like to do what's called the 'deep dive' and that can even be what's best for each individual. But like you Stella they will hopefully find their own seeds are just waiting in place. Always have been, you simply needed to allow them in."

As Yakazan shimmered Stella was nodding away feeling with some amusement that she was being what she called a noddy, when referring to those that stand behind politicians in televised interviews nodding at everything that is said. She often wondered what would happen if they stood shaking their heads in disagreement. Amused once more on where her thoughts were taking her, she brought them back to this special time with Yakazan.

"Lots of amusing thoughts floating through my mind Yakazan and along with them came an old saying 'one man's treasure may be another's trash 'and vice versa. It's reassuring to know that what is considered a treasure and worth having doesn't only operate on the level of material possessions but also in a spiritual sense. And what I treasure about myself certainly doesn't mean I am more special than anyone else. I still hold the dream of how wonderful it would be if all of humans here on this planet could begin treasuring each other and start experimenting living from this point of view."

Yakazan's shimmer seemed to quiver with excitement. "Stella keep holding that dream as an intention. Speaking on behalf of all light beings scattered throughout the Universe. There would be great excitement and celebration to see Humans experimenting with getting along. Which could be more than a dream when humans finally realise that no one walks this planet alone. And neither are you alone in what you know of as your Milky Way. Yes, it is big but there are countless galaxies in the Universe, and beyond which are larger."

Resisting the urge to go into overwhelm about the sheer size of the Universe that Earth's scientists could only guess at, Stella, gave into the impulse to stand hoping that Yakazan would remain for a while longer and walk with her among what she personally called her tall and proud trees. As she stood, she could hear Barry singing out to her.

"There you are Stella, for a moment I wondered where you were but then those dazzling white shoes of yours caught my eye. Just wanted to let you know that I am a bit late starting dinner. So, you have probably another half hour maybe a bit more to enjoy what has got those shoes glowing so brightly."

Blowing Barry a kiss and waving to let him know that she had heard him, before she started to move, she couldn't resist a glance noticing for herself how dazzling her shoes were. *Magic at work once more* she thought with an equally dazzling smile.

"Stella you are definitely not alone on your earth walk and many are awakening and evolving, rather than continuing to adapt in order to survive. You know only too well the history of conflicts that humans keep repeating. An opportunity for change comes along and yet so many choose adapting rather than face the challenges of evolving. That failure to do so keeps conflict cycles repeating. Even you Stella kept adapting and changing to fit with other's point of view until in your own words 'woke up 'and then began evolving."

For a moment Stella couldn't help but think if more put their focus into evolving what a wonderful world it would indeed be. Everyone and the planet would benefit.

"Powerful thoughts Stella, keep spreading them around. But don't fall into the trap of judgement. You really can't walk in another's shoes or know what triggers them unless they share it with you. Humans are so diverse and will wake up on their own timelines. Would you be running for the hills away from my present shimmering form, if your expanded sense of self hadn't brought you to this place in time?

I happen to know that it was the tale of the Ugly Duckling which you thought best described you and your life while you were searching for where you fit. Yet here I am walking with you connecting along with you to the trees in your own backyard, enjoying the birdsong. Amazingly you took reconnecting with me, the Liquid Light Woman and all that was a part of our adventure in your stride. You welcomed, accepted, received and embodied the wisdom that was shared. Think of the Ugly Duckling, you related to, as an energy form and during our encounters you transformed into the energy form of a snowy white swan. Keep honouring that beautiful and powerful Truth of that energetic transformation."

Before she could completely absorb the message in Yakazan's words Stella, not only noticed the increase in those shimmers but could sense their heightened vibrations. She couldn't help but laugh herself as she figured that increase was Yakazan laughing which was confirmed when she heard her whisper.

"Psst Stella, it's not only magic that keeps your walking shoes snowy white. It's because you were ready and willing to accept that transformation. You could also call this chapter in your life book 'Power'. It is time to fully accept you already are who you have been seeking to be. As well as it being time to step forward into the power of that Truth. Not just to honour it but trust it more than ever before. Remembering, to embody something is to live it. "

Sensations of joy were flooding through Stella as Yakazan's words found a soft landing within her while at the same time she could sense that their telepathic link was stronger than on any of their previous connections. Vivid pictures of her time in the Trust Garden were floating through her mind. Watching them with her internal eyes reminded her to keep viewing trust as a powerful spiritual tool. One that would trigger her to accept her own spiritual and healing abilities. And one which enabled her to discern which guidance, when coming at her from many different directions, was the best one for her.

Acceptance wasn't just a word, she thought, *but a lifetime process that would aid her in continuing her earth journey in a forward motion.* She had come to accept that she *held the key to honouring herself without judgement of what has been and how it can be.*

"Stella, I do enjoy being linked to your thought processes and where they take you. The word process can never be overused in the sense that consciousness and all that it reveals isn't static or a place that you arrive. It continues throughout your entire earth walk and beyond. The word process can also be used to describe that oft repeated question that so many humans utter. 'What is my Truth?' and 'How do I express it?'

These sentences are simply thought processes that keep the mind of the thinker going round in circles. This is where your phrase 'stop it' will come in handy."

Those words prompted a quick response from Stella. "By you just saying that I can recall how tired my mind and then of course my body would get when that thought, and others like it would just go round and round in circles. The image of a dog chasing its tail comes to mind. Thanks for the reminder to simply say 'stop it', I do hope the time will come when I no longer need to think or utter those questions."

Stella sensed Yakazan moving closer to her, and it was as if her shimmering presence had arms because the sensation of being held filled her before hearing Yakazan's gentle voice soothe her.

"Stella no doubt you will still have questions that may cause moments of disquiet. I know I have said it often that those seeds you left in place aeons ago are no longer concealed from your view. You have harvested them, you remain connected to them, and they will continue to germinate within you. They will always support you and be of value in both times of lightness and stress. I stress again you have harvested your own seeds. You were the one with the key, no one else could have opened your seeds. Only you could activate them. And you cannot open or harvest those belonging to another.

Putting talk of seeds and keys aside for the moment and because you are beginning to live with a more conscious awareness, I have a question for you. Have, you noticed Stella when you switch between your physical and spiritual reality how seamless that change is for you? And have you noticed how at ease you feel when both realities unite?"

A smile crossed her face as she was filled with the warmth of Yakazan's embrace along with the sensation of levitating. "Thank you I hadn't put what I have been experiencing into those words. It just feels like the new normal for me. Thank you again for turning up today in your beautiful, spectacular way and in right timing. Even knowing what I know, over the last few days I have had that feeling of being lost and questioning which path to walk again. Fortunately, I understand that sense of lostness sometimes turns up before another shift in perception."

"Stella, I hear your mind's question 'is my sharing this moment in time with you a coincidence or synchronicity?' What would your heart answer?"

"My heart answers synchronicity and I think I have just answered my own question. Whether my mind calls them crossroads or paths. My heart also has a mind which understands that the questioning allows time for a pause that presents me with the opportunity to get clear on my choices and whether they bring more joy into my daily life."

"Yes, Stella we are in sync and that pause you speak of is not static or bleak it's filled with divine energy. There are so many rich metaphors I could use. For example, being in an art gallery filled with magnificent paintings and you don't know where to look. But then you make a start pausing in front of one to take in all it is revealing to you before moving on to another. In this, fashion art imitates life as one step then the next step keeps you moving in a forward motion, laying the foundations to live the life you choose.

Or you may think of yourself as the singer of a musical score able to connect with a wide variety of notes and themes that raise your vibrations. You are the singer and your life with its bonds to Truth and to Love are your song. Your singer self can then become the dancer as well. Dancing to the rhythm of the tune your sounds create. A dance that enables you to remain steadfast in your power and flow with the challenges that still beset humans and not be flattened by what any changes bring.

A lot of words I know Stella to say that pauses are ok and can come with a beauty worth exploring."

Stella could feel gentle tears forming in her eyes again." This seems to be an afternoon for tears of joy. I am absorbing your words and looking forward to exploring and experiencing adventures rather than waiting for my earth years to come to an end. Your words, Yakazan, paint a picture that inspires me to affirm again that I am the choice maker on 'what sort of life am I sentencing myself to?' And I love the image of being a singer, and that my life is my song and I also get to choregraph the dance steps be they fast or slow. I feel full of overbubbling joy like the fizz that erupts from a champagne bottle especially when it's been shaken. Yes, that describes my sensation in this moment shaken, but in a good way. All that is not joyful, shaken loose."

"Ahh Stella, you may liken your shaken to my shimmer and I am reminded that what is a length of time for you is only momentary for me. And that's not to take away from the depth of our connection which is as valuable and affirming for me as it is for you. Right now, in both my moment and yours it feels appropriate to fade away. Leaving means I can return and share another measure of time with you. I honour and thank you. Rejoice that your harvest has borne fruit and enjoy what remains of this evenings' light and keep your eyes open for another shimmer or two."

Another shimmering embrace surrounded her, and as she melted into it her own laughter grounded her before hearing the familiar voice whisper in her ear "enjoy your dinner, I can smell it's rich aroma from here."

Yakazan was right, before she even set foot in the kitchen her sense of smell was greeted by a delicious aroma which tantalised her taste buds followed by surprise that Barry was nowhere in sight. Before curiosity about his whereabouts could take hold, Barry was making his way out of their bedroom obviously fresh from a shower.

"There you are Stella. Dinner won't be long. While I was showering a comforting thought passed through my mind. I do love how many solutions to any fears are washed away under the cleansing spray. And my fears that you may get lost somewhere 'out there' are finally at rest. I worked out that those shoes of yours are like beacons that will always guide you and ground you back here."

"Aww Barry I am so happy you can put those fears to rest. That's good news indeed it's good to be free of such concerns. I will go wash my hands. Then over dinner I can share what magic is afoot that keeps these shoes clean."

That unintended pun had Barry laughing "Ok Stella, can't wait to hear more and as you have noticed before there will be no eye rolls from me. There is something else we need to decide on. Mavis and Garry phoned today asking if we would like to travel in convoy with them down the South Coast into Victoria. He is going to email me the list of national parks and coastlines they intend to explore. When he sends it, we can talk further but the proposed dates he has already mentioned won't interfere with our trip to New Zealand."

Before dishing up her portion Stella took another moment to appreciate the delicious aromas emanating from the large skillet. "This looks so colourful Barry. Let's talk about magic, dates and plans when we are finished eating. This divine new recipe of yours is worthy of our full attention. Oh, Barry, I bet it tastes as good as it looks. I do look forward to our after-dinner conversation. But can't wait to say that I am finally beginning to understand that I am ready to explore living life without the pressure of 'I have to 'or the tyranny of the 'shoulds'. I thought I was making good choices but was sometimes aware of an inner resistance to living life fully. Though I am still exploring what it fully means I have this sense running through me of what freedom must feel like. I am finally committed to the adventure of enjoying life as it is now and what's to come."

Barry, Stella noticed had another big smile on his face." That's like hearing good news, I know you have struggled a bit with how to move forward while at the same time I recognise you have so much to share. And the timing of when that happens will suit you without caving into the pressure of others and yourself. Now let's eat."

A full heart comes with a beautiful mind.
Ra Lu Ca

Two years later

CASSIE

Angelic Time Out

She knew Stella wasn't attending this retreat with her and Josh. Nevertheless, for some reason she thought she might see her walking these rustic hallways once again. She even took a moment to sit in the chapel where together they had experienced some beautiful moments.

Perhaps reliving those memories was what was keeping Stella's energy close.

Cassie was rather bemused by her own thinking because she knew that Stella was in New Zealand with Barry. They had spoken that morning. This was Stella and Barry's second trip there in recent years. A group of therapists kept inviting her over the Tasman to facilitate mentoring days. Cassie wasn't surprised by that at all as Stella had so much to give not only treatment techniques but how to listen not only to the clients' words but to their body as well. Even though her own work wasn't hands on she had learnt much from Stella herself and it had become automatic to intentionally create a sacred space for both her and her client whether in person or online.

Stella would often run ideas by her to see if they made any earthly sense. 'Just checking', she would always say as she was open about having her head in the clouds while making the effort to keep her feet on the ground. Stella's approach to spirituality was practical, one which added to and made a difference in how she lived each day. And even if it hadn't been Stella's intention. It had become an approach that both her and Josh sought to apply to their lives.

Josh and herself had planned this three-day weekend away, not on the spur of the moment that had marked their previous attendance. Young Stella was staying with Josh's parents. Then just for a moment Cassie felt a twinge of sorrow remembering the events that had led to their previous presence at this retreat. She was happy to note that gazing at the gardens visible through the doors and windows once again had a soothing and calming effect on her.

Life was very different this time round. For one she was a very fit and healthy twenty weeks pregnant, and they had found out that morning they were expecting a boy. They had decided that before this welcome addition to their family arrived, they would take advantage of this weekend being just for them. The promo for this retreat came at the right time for them to participate because the following weekend they were off on a family beach holiday. *But that was a week away* she thought before bringing her attention back to their decision to attend this retreat. Before coming they had discussed how they were both looking forward to Crow's wise guidance and connecting again with the Angels in a tangible way. And had shared with each other their similar intentions to deepen and expand on the energy they had experienced last time at this incredible venue.

Happy shivers of excitement ran through her and hearing the dinner bell, was more than happy to leave her musings and join Josh in the dining room for the Friday evening welcome dinner. Before she could make her way in that direction Josh was by her side, and she stepped into his hug.

"Cassie, you seem a mite calmer and that serene pregnant glow I have gotten used to seeing on your face is back in full force. You aren't alone in how you feel. It was hard to leave our girl. But if her smiling face was any indication, she is going to have a fun time. We will call after dinner. Oh, and just a heads up, Crow was asking about Stella, and she didn't seem surprised that we named our daughter after her or that she continues to play a large role in our lives.

Now this may sound silly, but I keep expecting to see Stella pop up. Grown up Stella that is."

"Not silly at all Josh because I have been looking for her too. She will laugh when I share that with her. But who knows Stella may just be able to be in two places at once. At least energetically. She had been happy to hear that we had booked in for this retreat. Now take my hand and lead me to this feast."

Their phone calls with their precious daughter last night and this morning had allayed any fears that she was missing them. Knowing this, helped both her and Josh to soak up and settle into the calm peaceful flow of the retreat. And from all accounts Josh's parents were having as much fun as she was. Their baby girl was growing up but hopefully not too fast. At only two years old she was quite a chatterer and loved to just sit and chat. She appeared to be excited about the changes that were ahead for their family, but they also knew that she would only fully grasp what that meant when her brother finally arrived. They kept their fingers crossed the reality wouldn't cause too many dramas.

When they had last attended this retreat both herself and Josh enjoyed the easy way that Crow had of imparting the pearls of wisdom that effortlessly flowed through her. This relaxed manner had made it easy to absorb the insights that she relayed to the group. Once again Crow was encouraging them to strengthen their existing relationships with their Angelic Teams. Reminding them that Angelic guidance was always available to help in all life situations, advising them not to forget that they only needed to ask for their guidance and assistance. Without any sense of judgement Crow admonished them not to fall into complacency and doubt the role that the Angels could play in their lives. There were two key words she advised them to stay connected to, *invite* *and allow*. *That seemed such a simple thing to do,* thought Cassie, and recalled for a few moments when she had followed through on asking the Angels for help. On those occasions she had put the situation or feelings of concern into their loving hands, and remembered how she was always amazed by their quick response and resolution. Sadly, she also recalled the times when life's hustle and bustle often brought forgetfulness, when challenges and upsets were suffered before remembering to ask, invite and allow. She really did wish to stop forgetting and keep remembering.

During the session before lunch Crow asked them to focus on connecting with their hearts and visualise the love space that was present within that area of their body. Using the word allow again she directed them to "open and allow your heart and heart chakra to receive love, breathe in the phrase 'I am love' and accept that in that moment and every moment you are love." After, repeating that a few times she went on to reassure them. "By opening to more love, it doesn't mean that you have to keep giving out more love. Activating and holding the space of self-love within your own hearts, Love will naturally emanate from you and will cease to be a transaction or a love that puts conditions on another."

It wasn't entirely new information Cassie thought, but Crow had framed it in such a way that it brought self-love into the now, attainable, not something to wait for or to come from the future.

The repetition of 'I am Love,' flowed softly through her and she could sense a rise in her own eagerness to hear what else Crow had to say.

"Think of your heart space as your heart mind. It is not your brain, that responds to feelings and situations first. Your heart does. Keep in mind that it's not only the electrical impulse centre of your body but the emotional centre as well. Thoughts and feelings in this sense are not separate but exist together. Feelings arrive with the thought. It's time to bring the thoughts that lodge and sometimes get stuck in your busy heads into your hearts. We've all been told at one time or another to use our brains and think before we act and that may have served you in the past, but this is the time to switch yourselves on to listening to your hearts.

Accept how you are feeling. And that means all of your feelings don't push the ones you would rather ignore away. Even what you call a negative feeling can lead to healing and adding more love to your day.

Yes, you will still use those beautiful brains, they are not going anywhere. Listening to your heart enables you to think, speak and act from the love space you have created. And guides you to the understanding that love is an energy; it never leaves you. You might leave it for a time, and when you notice that is happening you simply need to tune back into love because it's like a musical score or theme that is playing in the background of your daily lives.

'Follow your heart', is a saying that is often said, and now's the time to follow yours and trust the choices that you make from your heart mind. Keep practicing and remembering that the power you have to love yourself, others and your ability to spread love around the world radiates from your heart mind."

Cassie could hear the smile in Crow's voice when she brought her words to a conclusion and just before lapsing into silence she added.

"And when in doubt 'Ask the Angels', they will hear you as they never sleep. "

Dropping into the love space within her heart, or what she now thought of as her heart mind, she opened her eyes briefly and was captivated by the look of bliss on Josh's face. For a moment she tuned into the surrounding silence that was only punctuated by the sounds of nature coming in through the open doors and windows. With eyes closed once more she repeated the words "to trust the choices that you make from your heart mind". They too flowed smoothly through her before she converted it to a personalised mantra. "I trust the choices that I make from love and my heart mind."

Along with the warm feeling of love flowing through her she had an image arise of pathways and journeys she had yet to take and sent love on the road ahead of her and then sent it back to the road behind her. "To trust the choices" made in love was a good practice to put into action she thought.

One she could commit to. In the years to come she wanted to be able to look back and view her life through the eyes of love, not ones filled with regret. Her focus was distracted by two frequently used cliched phrases, 'Rome wasn't built in a day.' `And 'practice makes perfect.'

Much used phrases and words that could use a little tweaking she thought, but yes, she could continue to evolve without rushing, there was no race she needed to win. And what was perfect for her was her ability and desire to create practices or rituals that added to her days, not detracted.

The distraction of these phrases was replaced with a feeling of contentment as she realised that both her and Josh had already laid the foundations for a loving and trusting relationship with each other, one which they both valued, and yet at the same time recognising the importance of building a loving and self-caring relationship with and for themselves. Love, she thought, leads to love, and at last, understood she needed to be the love of her life, and it was the same for Josh, that he needed to be the love of his life. *Bringing this self-love into their relationship* she further thought, could only enhance and strengthen the love they had for one another. She decided she quite liked that phrase, love leads to love. She hoped she would remember that when those sometimes-pesky daily challenges arose.

Amazingly Sunday rolled around seemingly on the flow of Angel wings. Last night's dinner had been such a Love feast as well as one of healthy food. And during this morning's facetime with their Stella, she was jumping up and down with excitement mentioning that she had so much to tell them. Wouldn't be much longer until she could.

She had felt excited herself going into the morning sessions and looked forward to setting some clear take home intentions. There would be time on the way home or during next couple of days for Josh to share his own thoughts. She hadn't booked in any clients and Josh wasn't going into work until the following Wednesday when he would finalise what needed to be attended to before heading to the beach. That he'd carved out that time to turn their weekend into a long weekend had been a welcome surprise and she now looked forward to having that time with each other and of course young Stella.

But right now, she decided to make another visit to the chapel while Josh had gravitated to kitchen duty again. This time he was helping to set out the farewell lunch. *Rather a hallmark of his professional self* she thought with a smile, to be there at both the beginning and completion. A desire for continuity was also a word that could be applied to how Josh operated in the world. She was more than happy to spend these moments enjoying the chapels' peaceful atmosphere. In this quiet space she could hear the echoes of the conversation she had with Stella a few years ago. Those memories were etched so vividly in her mind that it felt as though it had only happened yesterday.

With a smile she allowed those earlier memories in her mind to be replaced by one of their most recent conversations about life's crossroads. Which was often a subject of discussion for them. The words Stella used in their last conversation, before she'd headed off to New Zealand, were making more sense. Yes, they had decided however spiritually evolved they were, life would be filled with challenges and what might sometimes feel like being at crossroads. But as was the way of many of their conversations Stella's words flowed gently with a proviso, they were her thoughts put into words and she didn't require others to think the same as her. More times than not her words were like shiny gems that resonated and clarified her own thought processes. Even with her pregnancy brain she could recall Stella's words.

"Crossroads aren't about going anywhere. This way or that way. They are about how to be more Love, how to raise my light vibrations and how to create more joy. They allow me to stop and pause for a moment, especially if life doesn't seem to be going well. It's a pause that grants me the opportunity and if necessary to choose again. To allow love to be my guide."

If Stella was here, she'd also affirm once more that these ideas were "only true for her and may not be true for another." Thinking back on Stella's words strengthened her commitment to her intention to open her own heart and continue to invite and allow love to flow through her. She had the sense that the power of that love would support her in all areas of her life. One that she could use like a bright light to shine on some aspects of herself that were way past time to be released. As well as shining a light on what aspects of herself she needed to develop and grow into. *What an adventure she was embarking on,* she thought, and was more than optimistic that hers and Josh's own adventure would often coincide. They may take different pathways but how fortunate they were that they would be able share and hold hands along the way.

Hearing the dinner bell brought her focus back to the practicalities of life, proclaiming to herself that while she loved these moments of recollection and reflection, she also loved the idea of heading towards lunch, knowing already without sighting it, that she was going to love the food and company to share it with. *Love* she laughed to herself *was as simple as that in everyday life.*

For a weekend that had stretched out before them it hardly seemed possible that it was now time for a group photo bringing all that they discovered and discussed together to a heartfelt conclusion. And was followed by sharing warm hugs filled with gratitude and meaningful well wishes before scattering to their cars to make their journeys home. Cassie was pleased that she and Josh didn't need to make any detours and could go straight home. Josh's parents had volunteered to take their beautiful daughter home to their place to await their arrival. His parents were thoughtful in so many ways.

As always it was a delight to drive through the countryside and absorb the peace and quiet before hitting the busy highway. Breaking the comfortable silence Cassie thanked Josh once more for taking a couple of days off while also understanding that he still needed to put in some work hours.

"Josh I am so grateful that we have the next couple of days together. Have I said lately how amazing it is that you are achieving a healthy work life balance. You not only came up with a plan, but you put it into action. And I love you for it not only for myself but for you as well. You have worked hard for so many years and it's great to witness that the fruits of your labours are working for you and not against you."

"Aww sweet Cassie I am happy that you have stuck with me through all the long hours until I could put what both Jeff and I intended when we started our firm into place. What is really great is that as partners we have always been on the same page. We knew starting out, as did you and Amy before her and Jeff were married, that building a reputable architectural firm was not for the faint hearted. In those early stages we couldn't be anything but fully involved from start to completion for work that came our way. Your unwavering support meant as much to me as did the successful conclusions to those projects. Which in turn, added more projects and long hours. You know only too well how important it is to build and maintain a trusted reputation."

Cassie couldn't hold back her smiles as she put her thoughts into words." I am so proud of all you have achieved; you and Jeff deserved every success. My heart feels warm and full to know that you are both still on the same page about making the changes in your workplace. And it won't be long now until Jeff experiences becoming a first time father. Has he been asking you for any tips?

"A few Cassie, he remembers the sleep deprivation our beautiful daughter generated but accepts it goes along with welcoming a child into the world. He and Amy will be great parents and are both excited. He has a calendar on the wall separate from work projects as they count down the weeks. Luckily, we will get in our beach holiday before their baby arrives and he has time off. Then when it's the second time around for us he will be back in good time for me to be home with you and our babies. I am so excited our family is growing. But I go back to what I said earlier, and we have discussed, starting out we knew if we put in the hours and earned a good reputation for our innovative and good work practices we would get to a place where we could employ other talented architects and appoint an office manager who would handle all that's involved in researching and tendering for projects. While we may still steer the ship and keep our eyes on projects, we are happy to not control every aspect of our workplace. We welcome creative ideas and discussions. It's a great space to be in knowing that we can step back a bit, have holidays and take time off. Our trust in those we now employ is rewarded by their loyalty."

It wasn't long before they pulled into their driveway. Then felt bemused that their daughter who earlier that morning had been so eager to see them, wasn't bounding out of the house to greet them. And were instead being greeted by her grandparents.

"Thanks mum and dad but where's our girl?" Josh exclaimed.

"I think she wishes to surprise you with her packing prowess".

Cassie and Josh looked at each other rather mystified.

Seeing that expression Therese continued with a smile in her voice.

"Your delightful chatterbox has kept us well entertained this weekend. What has filled us with wonder though isn't that she talks so well but that she has complete comprehension of what she says and the expressions she hears."

"Mum, we don't call her 'little miss big ears' for nothing. So, what's she packing?"

"When your dad and I noticed she was no longer looking out the window waiting for your arrival we found her in her bedroom. She'd had a soft bag on her bed and was rummaging through her draws while deciding what to pack in her bag. When we asked her what she was doing we were both so surprised."

"Therese, Tom." Cassie jumped in "I think I know what you are going to say but please go on."

"I think we should have recorded it, but this is the gist of her reply. 'I am looking for all my light, bright and easy clothes to pack Gran and Gramps. Did you know that some people carry heavy suitcases all through life? Not ever taking the heavy stuff out. I heard mum and dad talking about it. And do you know that leaves no room for the lighter and happy things? For our holiday I am only packing my happy, fun things. My bag will be light. I can leave a jacket, like mum and dad do in the car in case I need it!'"

"Ahh little miss big ears did indeed hear and knows how to put a plan into action. One minute Josh and I were talking about making lists for what we needed to pack for our holiday which seemed to naturally flow into talking about life and the baggage we carry. We then fell into discussing what is supportive and about what actually gets in the way and is unnecessary. I posed the question 'if we came across a river, whose opposite side offered a new way of being and an opportunity to look with new eyes. Would we want to get to the other side?' Then once deciding yes, finding out that the only way to cross was by steppingstones that could only support a certain weight. What would we jettison from our suitcases?

What would we choose to take out to lighten any load so we could experience the love, joy, peace and harmony on the other side? She may understand heaps, but I don't think she quite gets what metaphors are."

Shaking his head Josh reached out to take her hand to draw her through the front door. "Come on Cassie, our girl seems to know what works for her, can't wait to see what she's packed. Let's go and find out and get those hugs we have been hanging out for."

Three things that cannot be long hidden:
the sun, the moon, and the truth.
Buddha

STELLA

The Viewing Point

Stella's phone rang just as they pulled into yet another scenic lookout. Though she couldn't wait to get out of their hired campervan and join Barry at this viewing point. She took a moment to take in Cassie's call and laugh at young Stella's antics and her own delight again in being called Big Stella. *Being called Big Stella never got old,* she thought and would enjoy it while she could. Knowing that in the years ahead and if the height of her mum and dad was any indication her namesake would shoot up, bypassing her own short stature. No more 'Big Stella 'then. Which is exactly what her own grandchildren had done. For years it had seemed that her precious grandchildren's main goal in life had been to be taller than their grandmother. She was now relegated to being the shortest in the family and more than happy that they had all achieved their goal.

On the completion of her workshops, they had set off on this much anticipated tour of New Zealand's South Island. Last time here they'd explored the North Island. While she was otherwise occupied Barry had poured over maps, and followed up on the suggestions about what not to miss, that the participants had shared with her during workshop breaks. Each route so far had lived up to the descriptions of what the maps and brochures had described as being the best scenic routes. Best was a relative term she thought as each turn in the road was what she and Barry called a Kodak moment. *She was living firsthand,* she thought, Yakazan's words about being in an art gallery and that feeling of overwhelm of not knowing where to look first. They soon realised as they were meandered along, that they couldn't stop around every corner, or their journey would take far more time than they had allowed. This latest stop was going to be a morning tea stop as well.

Drinking in the surrounding spectacular scenery at each stop always filled her eyes with tears and her heart with an incredible joy. The majesty and might could have been overwhelming but instead, it gifted her with a sense of her own place and role as a speck of light that could radiate throughout the Universe. And being a speck didn't make her feel small or diminished in any way. Expanded, was the word which best described her sense of being one with and at the same time part of her surroundings and the entire Universe.

Besides the scenery's inspiring impact, she had noticed numerous liberating thoughts floating through her mind. Her present thoughts confirmed how far she had moved beyond the cage of her own making to the freedom to create her own life. Her life was based on her choices. She knew without doubt that when they returned home, those oft-quoted words 'all good things must come to an end, 'wouldn't be true. They couldn't be true as she would always carry the imprint of the energy and joy generated by the awe-inspiring terrain of this beautiful country. And it struck her that it worked both ways. Her deep breaths in and out carried in them molecules and an energy that was just her. It was a comforting thought that because of her breaths that a part of her would remain as energetic whispers leaving her imprint in nature, and wherever her earth walk had taken her. As well with those who had passed through her life.

Smiling to herself she became aware that her imagination wasn't going to take a back seat to her philosophical ruminations. For she found herself imagining that if humans took a moment each morning to map out a day filled with joy. They could deal with whatever challenges unfolded. And when dealt with be able to return to joy knowing that the imprint of that joy remained. She was keeping her fingers crossed that she had left behind judging herself for what she referred to as her fanciful thoughts, because they were ones she wished to live by.

One thing she knew she could do well was to laugh at herself and found herself casting her mind back to her earlier concerns about crossroads. Yes, she viewed them differently now. But back then if she had a greater understanding about where her present thoughts had taken her, she wouldn't have been dithering filled with concerns and anxieties regarding which path to take. Thankfully she now knew that whatever path she took she could create joy. Now she could take that one step further celebrating that the imprint of her joy remains. *And why stop there* she thought the imprint of love and being light also remains.

She was doing it again, what her mother called wool gathering. *Only good wool*, she thought before finally alighting from the van, to make her way quietly to Barry's side. Taking his hand, she matched his reverent silence as together they beheld this sublime view laid out before them. The sun was out, shining brightly in the bluest of skies and the breeze was light with only a hint of chill. Majestic, magnificent were the most common words they often used to describe the views they had witnessed. Earlier on their road trip and at other viewing points Stella had stopped trying to find other adjectives but now in this place and in this moment, she mentally added magical and mystical. In the magic of this place, she found herself feeling emotional again as she inwardly looked back recalling the beauty they had passed through before bringing her full attention back to feasting her eyes again on the ruggedness of the landscape and the snow-capped mountains that were now laid out before them. Anticipation for what wonders still lay ahead was also taking up some space in her thoughts.

"Barry, I don't like breaking the silence." She whispered. "It seems almost disrespectful and yet at the same time appropriate in this sacred space to share a couple of the thoughts that are traveling through my mind. One, I am so happy we have made this trip. And two, as I look out at all this magnificence and revisit in my mind what we have already witnessed I have to wonder if what we are experiencing is a good metaphor for life."

Barry squeezed her hand while commenting quietly." Stella I always love to hear your thoughts. I know you often say you are being fanciful, but your words always make sense to me. Go ahead you have me curious now."

"Well, here we are at a place or moment in time where I feel as though we are on top of the world. We can look back and catch glimpses of the beauty along the road we have just travelled. That's the metaphor I would like to apply to my emotional journey and know it can be as simple as looking back without regrets and truly love all that's ever been, all of my creations. Doing so activates those seeds of mine. I know you remember Barry when I shared the story of those seeds' courage, willingness and trust with you. Though they don't just belong to me they are seeds everyone can access and put to use in whatever way is meaningful for them.

Courage to cease holding on to my own limiting beliefs and judging myself. Courage to realise that the only effort required is my willingness to continue healing and transforming old and even new hurts and wounds. Trust is always a biggie for me and know the more trust I embody the more I can love what's in the past, in the now and send love before me."

"I agree Stella this moment and the beauty of this spot inspires me to look back and see, however it appeared at the time, that my life has been an adventure. But more and more I find it inside me rather than seeking for it on the outside. Remember those children's books 'Choose Your Own Adventure.' You would get so far in the story then be presented with different page numbers to go to and that would change the story outcomes.

Well, that's me but I see it more like baking a cake. Choosing the best ingredients for each cake. The tastes and textures may vary but still have delightful outcomes and the icing on the cake, excuse the pun, is sharing the outcomes of my adventure with you. Love doing that as much as you love sharing your internal adventures with me."

"Mountain tops really are magical for me Barry, so many times during meditation I visualise myself on a the top of mountain. Right now, though I feel as though I could joyfully jump off into the unknown without any fear."

Feeling a firmer squeeze from Barry's hand Stella laughed.

"Don't worry Barry, my wings haven't been serviced lately so I am not going to. Not before morning tea anyway."

"Stella I can feel excitement vibrating through you. Being surrounded by such magnificence inspires me to commit to staying excited about the road ahead. And by that I don't only mean travelling like we are now but also at home. How wonderous to feel excited rather than fearing the unknown."

Revealing Insights

They set up a small table and fold up chairs next to their van and over morning tea Stella brought the phrase 'fear of the unknown' back into their conversation.

"Barry following up on what you said about fearing the unknown I think I have finally 'got this' the 'this' I am supposed to get. Now don't laugh I can see you are about to."

Raising his arms in surrender "I will not laugh." Then proceeded to do so." Stella I am not laughing at you but am amused, especially as that phrase 'got this' has bugged you for so long. But I do wish to hear what you have to say. Before you do, I must say considering the traffic that's been flowing along this road it's amazing that no one has stopped to take in this view. It's great to have it to ourselves."

"Yes, Barry having this place to ourselves is wonderful indeed. Now let me see if I can tease this idea of mine into making sense. Fear is a normal reaction to getting out of the way of traffic or something falling on us, or a sudden noise and sometimes we fear outcomes. It's become normal to throw fear and the unknown together. And it is valid in the case of waiting for results of medical tests and other life issues.

But now I am going to put it with fearing our unknown selves. I am going to use the term 'we', but I realise and say this without judgement that not everyone chooses to do so. For those of us that do set out on our own spiritual and emotional journeys, we start to remember bit by bit that we are love, and light and all that good stuff. When we start out, we are searching and yes, all that good stuff become ideals to aspire to. To truly live being our real selves of pure love, light, joy and again all that comes with it is what was unknown when we each set off on those journeys.

This is where I am trying to make sense in words of an awareness and it's hard to match words to it. Stepping past the awareness stage and moving into action brings with it questions to answer and unravel. Is it the unknown me that I have always strived to be that I fear? And if so, what is that fear about? What, is it I really fear? Is it how will I be, will I be different? What would my life look like when I live each day knowing that the energy of pure love, light joy and peace is at the core of my very being.? Can I sustain living and embodying this understanding? Will I trust my transformation and fully step out of having human doubts? Will I continue to dabble my toes in the river of life, or immerse my whole foot completely?"

Barry, who had been listening attentively to her words had a gentle smile forming on his face before breaking the silence that had followed Stella's sharing.

"Mmmm, Stella if I am following you correctly then stepping into all the good stuff, to use your words, is what has been unknown to us. And the fear being can we step into it and live it? Makes us humans a kind of crazy lot if we choose not to. From my perspective maybe we should focus on raising our trust levels. Doubts are normal I think, they come, and they go. You know what I am like when I doubt whether a new recipe is going to work or you Stella when you swing back and forth on what you will wear when we go somewhere. I have noticed that you usually go back to your first choice. What we are doing though is not trusting ourselves. We are doing all that swinging in and out of doubt without knowing or paying enough attention to its effects. Going back to what you shared earlier I would add when we fully trust ourselves, we wouldn't fear being our true selves when we fully trust we're ok as we are.

The slight chill that had been in the air gave way to a warmth and taking Stella's hand again Barry found he had more to add.

"I think the practice of checking in daily to notice if there are doubts lingering around could be another mission or a purpose, we both can share. Rather than deny doubts or push them away, we can accept them as normal. Can only release them when we notice them. Maybe then even if it's not at the same time, immerse a foot in fact both feet into the flow of that river of life."

Although they could hear the sound of passing traffic, they still had this glorious location to themselves the *perfection of this spot* Stella thought served to add energy to their insightful conversation.

"Barry, I think we have just found new chapters to explore and add to each of our life books. Perhaps we could call the chapter being real and accepting our true selves."

"Luckily for us we can laugh at ourselves and with each other because that's a long title. Right now, Stella there's a smooth rock over there in front of the barrier and there appears to be a brighter patch of sunshine there. I will put away our morning tea paraphernalia then check the map once more. Why don't you go over and sit while I do so. It looks just meant for you."

"Why thanks Barry, is that so I don't see you eat that last slice of cake?"

"You know me well, but not entirely, it just seems like it's calling you. But I'll say it again, do me a favour, don't go test driving those wings here."

Laughing while she made her way to the rock Barry had pointed out to her she was already beginning to feel the shimmer and vibration which heralded Yakazan's arrival. And after the conversation she and Barry had just had she was sure Yakazan also had something to contribute. She could hear Yakazan's chuckle before that gentle and always soothing voice began to speak quietly to her.

"I think I know why your chuckle precedes any wisdom you wish to impart." And as always, an increase in the vibration of the shimmer was a sign that the chuckle had turned into Yakazan's version of laughter.

"Ahh Stella I am laughing with you and with great joy at how beautifully and gracefully you are becoming who you are. Not just words but truly becoming. Sure, you are aware that you've 'got this' can still be challenged by life events. And even if understanding the previously unknown fear is an idea that's still unraveling at present. It's bringing you to a point of acceptance, where you can embrace who you were before beginning your Earth walk. You have taken so many steps to get this to place."

For a moment they sat together in this patch of light, absorbing the warmth of it before Yakazan continued. Stella knew Yakazan always had more to say and welcomed her words.

"Stella let's travel back in time. As you began your Earth walk there was much that was unknown to you. Fear as you know only too well became part of your human cycle because as children, then as adults you learnt there were things to fear and distrust. Often the fears and lack of trust was that of others. We have had many conversations about that. As you have discovered many times the unknown remains unknown until you know it. In this case what has made itself known is that your fear of being your Real self sometimes overtakes you and prevents you from and basking in your brilliance. Add to your knowing this idea, instead of making being human a chore, see yourself in the light of all you have accomplished in your human form as being brilliant."

Conversations with Yakazan, she thought, *always aided her in unlearning any lingering old beliefs and re learn how to create new thoughts and intentions that as Barry had hinted at would make a greater difference in their lives.*

She gave herself a slight shake of delight as she felt the impact of Yakazan's presence and her words creating a tingling sensation in the region of her solar plexus which was quickly spreading throughout her whole body.

"Humans, brilliant as you are, like to talk about the weather which is a good metaphor for the life journeys you undertake. At any stage of your evolution when you leave unsupportive beliefs and behaviour patterns behind, there is a period of adjustment that may or may not take time. You are acclimatising in the same way that when your seasons change, especially from warm weather to sudden cold snaps and vice versa, you need time to catch your breath for you to adjust. A rest may be in order as you get used to the new season before it begins to feel like a good fit."

"I must confess once upon a time I ignored my body's need to rest and would incorrectly view myself as weak. But now I finally see the value of rest especially knowing that my physical body is going through a period of readjustment created by an increase in my energetic frequency and soul vibrations. I don't have to run to keep up but can take it easy, and at the same time remember how important grounding is along with aligning the higher frequencies coursing through my body, mind and soul. I feel fortunate that I have come to understand my physical reactions to energetic shifts occurring throughout the Universe. Wouldn't like to still be in the dark about it and stuck in wondering what's wrong with me. Am so over thinking *something's wrong with me."*

"Like I said earlier Stella, humans are brilliant and that's wonderful that you have grown in this understanding and no longer find ways to make yourself wrong. We still have our telepathic link, but I respect your space Stella to live and grow your way, therefore I am not always tuning in, only in times like now or when I sense your need of some direction. Having said that I did hear you say that you are a 'speck of light.' I suggest that you do a little tweaking and see yourself as a point of bright light. One so bright that it radiates in all directions connecting you to other points of light. This light has never been a destination it's always been inside you. That's what makes humans multidimension beings whether or not individuals can embrace that concept."

Stella felt those words resonate within her in the same way that her earlier sensation of being part of everything and everything being part of her had.

"It's also good to hear Stella that you now know the value of rest because your human vessel houses your light body, and your light body houses your Soul. Taking care of yourself is important on many levels. Barry was spot on, when he spoke of you both raising your trust levels. Stella, do you doubt you have a soul? Do you doubt the Creator exists or the Universe of the Creator? Do you doubt yourself?"

"A lot to ponder there Yakazan." She thought for a moment and took a deep breath as she considered her answers" I don't doubt that I have a Soul and I don't doubt the Creator or that the Creator's Universe exists. I must amend that because as I was saying those words, I realised I can still fall into my old trap of thinking that I just have a vivid imagination. Fortunately, not as often and only turns up as a thought when I doubt myself and my choices.

What would life be like if my trust was fully aligned with self-love, with my truth? This seems to be another example of how the unknown can become a lived known."

"Good answers Stella. We have travelled backwards in time now we are traveling forward to right now where you could think of it this way. Doubt is a part of the human mindset. Barry had a great idea of checking in daily to notice the presence of doubts. If you do so you can release them, and your trust levels will increase to a point where you will trust the truth of who you are and be able to live it. What would it look like?

But before you picture that I might add that Trust is a word that humans developed to know whether something feels right for you or not. It holds hands with your intuition. Before you ever were in this human vessel you simply knew. It's time to trust the part of you that knows."

Stella could accept that doubts could show up as an everyday common occurrence. To reverse this, she thought a good place to start would be to notice what she trusted rather than maintaining a focus on what she didn't trust. She realised that she trusted that the electrical appliances in her kitchen would work, that her car would start. That when she went shopping the supermarket would be in the same place as the last time she was there. That the sun would rise and set regardless of weather conditions. Perhaps silly examples but in viewing these simple things it was rather startling to realise that there was so much, she did trust. At this stage in her life, she decided it was time to put aside any lingering pesky doubts and fully trust herself and her feelings around trust. And trust it was safe to be her.

"Ahh, Stella from those thoughts of yours I can hear this is another 'this' you are getting."

It's fortunate she thought that she could laugh at herself when she considered how she could make something so simple, complex.

Yakazan's presence always filled her with warmth. Those tingles she felt earlier were still coursing through her and were also carrying with them a great sense of excitement about possible new individual chapters that her and Barry could step into.

"Stella another thing to consider as you take all this in, is that trusting your soul should always be your first priority and from there it will naturally spill over into all areas of your life. Including placing more trust in the Creator and the Universe of the Creator."

"Yakazan, I do hope I get to a place where when, looking back I wonder why I ever had doubts. But then as you say they are normal especially when attempting and adapting to new ways of experiencing life. Earlier Barry and I were joking about my wings. Are they still a symbol of my trust seed, as they were in the Trust Garden?"

"A good question Stella. Your wings will always be part of you. Unseen by many but I know you have felt them on numerous occasions. They remain with you and move you through all aspects of your earth life. When you attached your wings to the butterfly tree you recognised how handy the power of trust would be on your earth walk. At that time, you understood trust's relationship to your truth.

Trust those wings to fly you high or allow you to hover when you need to stay in a particular space. They can energetically flutter to release clutter. In this case it's doubts that creates the clutter. Whether your wings fly you high or low they will keep moving you forward, and often at a fast pace. You may have noticed shifts in your perception are swift, you don't stay stuck for long, because Stella you now only take on new ideas that resonate with you. Ones that make sense that can and do make a difference in your everyday life. It is time to fully use that freedom that comes with having wings. Barry will walk his own path and bring his own trust and truth together. There is much beauty in your relationship, even when the downs seem down. The beauty is that you confront and share your feelings with one another. You ground one another through a look or a touch."

Stella could feel the beauty in Yakazan's words, and her eyes were drawn back to taking in once more the beauty and magnificence of the surroundings. She hadn't thought of her wings as something so tangible and how to use them in the physical world. But then of course why not she thought? Symbols could be both useful and practical.

"Stella just as you and Barry pulled into this viewing point, your friend Cassie phoned sharing with you what Young Stella said about packing. It may seem like one of those many coincidences that pop up in life but fits in well where our conversation is heading."

"Well, it certainly was in sync with that saying, 'out of the mouths of babes.' And it was nice to hear not only Cassie's voice but her delight as she shared this tale. As well as an account of their retreat experience."

"More questions for you to explore Stella.

What will you put in your suitcase for your journey ahead? Will you stay on the stepping-stones? What harm could you come to if you immersed one foot at a time in the river?"

Before she could marshal her thoughts Yakazan had the answers for her.

"You don't need to pack light for that is what you already are. Nor love as again that is what you are. That has always been your truth. You don't even need to carry a suitcase. You are free to merge with your Soul's energy.

You have exercised your freedom to live a human experience.

The seeds you planted carried an energetic intention that flowed throughout your journey and that energy flow will be ongoing while you remain on your earth walk.

Exercise that freedom again as you continue your human experience and live as a consciously and integrated Soul infused personality. Your Soul's energy has and will remain what or who you truly are."

"They are powerful words Yakazan. Ones that are bubbling away and resonating with what has for many years been building in my awareness. I can't help but remember that in my early awakening stage I used to have the thought 'will someone please run up to me and tell what my truth is?' Because in my thoughts I had them running up to me, I must have been in a hurry."

She could feel Yakazan's chuckling shimmer before hearing her next words." You were often in a hurry, so it bodes well for your physical body to hear you saying earlier that you now know the value of rest and pacing yourself.

Humans tend to throw the words, 'their truth' around. Even you Stella say often 'while something may be true for you it doesn't automatically follow that it will be true for another. That is admirable but what you and others are sharing is your opinion. And each and every human has their own opinion on one subject or another and what sits best with them.

Being a Soul is the simple and basic truth for every human that has walked this planet or another word you fondly use is pure consciousness. This fundamental truth will never change and remains throughout all your timelines and throughout the Universe. When you complete this human experience, it is to that pure Soul energy you will return. "

"As I follow what you are saying, Yakazan the word purpose popped into in my mind. And as I am operating from a human perspective, I know I can still at times struggle with that word but have the sense that it is about to end. Rather like clouds parting in the sky, it is getting clearer that I can step into accepting that when I embarked on this life's experience it has been essential for me to arrive at this point in time to embrace and own my pure essence or soul energy and that when I am ready to complete this human experience without shying away from the words, Soul, Essence ,Source, Creator and Divinity I will simply Dissolve Into Energy. And know that my purpose is and always has been Love. To be love and loving all that exists.

I can feel goosebumps, ones of pleasure not cold. And am filled again with that sense of being part of everything and everywhere and finally clear that I am here to experience the joy and simplicity of that connection and my Soul's intention to know and be love."

"My goodness Stella you are getting this and more. You do enjoy your acronyms and Dissolve into Energy is spot on. Because you have graduated from past lengthy periods of transformation to ones of rapid change you may notice that feelings of overwhelm may sometimes make their presence felt."

"Yes, Yakazan I can definitely relate to feelings of overwhelm, and their presence is what triggered me to learn the value of rest that I mentioned earlier."

"Stella you may also consider that you have graduated from the school of striving to the school of Love. Even when the presence of love appears unlikely. When you no longer doubt yourself, or no longer deny how you feel in any given moment, is a form of Love, miracles happen every day and, in every moment, when you choose the energy of love. In a nutshell Love is your Soul's mission and what you always have been. Which makes your Soul's energy as essential to you as breathing. And that's what you are remembering now. Remembering has never been about focusing on the past it's remembering your unique Soul energy and to remind you that the Creator's presence, wisdom, light and love are within you."

"My goodness Yakazan that's a lot to unpack and I willingly embrace and embody all that you have spoken of. I actually feel excited and can envisage how clear the road ahead will be as I live, express and remember. Thank you Yakazan for reminding me. My wings have brought me to this place where I am truly safe and free to be me."

"Your wings Stella will always be guided by the frequency of love. And before you head off, I would like to add that while others may not see your wings. What they see is your joy. You spread it and help so many find joy. Stella your wings of joy are very effective. Some might say it's your superpower. See your laughing proves my point."

Stella couldn't help laughing and the following big smile as she thought of the idea of joy as her wings. It was an assuring and comfortable one.

"Joy is a quality to fully embody Stella. And it really is a great joy for me to spend this time with you. But it is getting time for you head off. Before you become concerned hardly any earth time has passed. We have been encapsulated in a bubble of light and I slowed down what is time for you. Our conversation may seem long and drawn out as we have covered many topics. I will burst the bubble soon but in Barry's reality enough time has passed for him to have that last piece of cake and he has almost finished his preparations for getting back on the road. It's my turn Stella to thank you for being so open to receiving love and my energy. I will see you somewhere along your road or on another mountaintop."

Stella once again experienced the warmth she associated with a Yakazan hug travelling through her body while also surrounding her. The sensation lingered for a moment before it slowly faded away.

Filled with joy and wonder Stella turned to see Barry packing up their folding chairs. She could hear his voice even though it sounded a long way away.

"Come on Stella, time to get back on the road."

Barry joined her when she was almost back at their vehicle giving her a big hug which brought her fully back to the present. And laughing they both burst into their travelling song 'On the road again.'

She was surprised when Barry asked. "What sort of life are we sentencing ourselves to?"

And they both laughed as they said at the same time. "Why that would be one of love, joy, fun and adventure."

"We've got this covered." Barry whispered. "Whether it be on the road or at home let's get to it and get going."

Helping Stella into the passenger seat Barry gasped when he looked down at Stella's shoes.

"Stella your shoes are brighter and a more dazzling white than the snow on the surrounding mountain peaks."

Their laughter which followed his surprised gasp and words echoed from those snowcapped peaks to the valleys, formed ripples on the lakes and energised the road ahead.

"Ahh so they are Barry." Stella said once their laughter had subsided. "And I feel as energised as they appear to be."

As they pulled out of the viewing spot what seemed like a convey of vehicles pulled in.

"Was that pure luck or meant to be? I am thinking Stella it has something to do with your shoes. Can't wait to hear about it over our evening meal."

"Yes, Barry as always, I will relieve your curiosity. But right now, the phrase from one of those hard sell television ads is flowing through my mind."

"I think I can guess that it's 'Wait there's more!'"

"Spot on Barry but I am not doing a sales pitch for 'Wait there's more.' I am thinking wait and there is always more. More light, love, joy and healing. We've got all angles covered all we need to do is keep going. Because there's no more waiting. No more hanging around for the right time to be open, receive and believe. No more digging for buried treasure. The time is now, we already are who we set out to be."

Which had Stella thinking and *so it is and forever will be.*

The End.

About the Author

Patricia Lovell has worn many hats during her earth walk. She is a wife, mother, stepmother, and grandmother and lives with her husband Brian in the beautiful Lake Macquarie area of New South Wales. While she doesn't have any pets, she is surrounded by colourful bird life and much to her amusement the possums have races on her roof.

One of her hats was that of a Remedial Massage Therapist. One she wore proudly after years of training in many healing modalities. She is sort of semi-retired. But remains happy to treat the small number of clients who still seek out her healing touch. And to her great joy her previous Remedial Massage teacher hat gets an outing when she regularly mentors new and experienced therapists.

And as she walked her own path, another hat she treasured wearing was facilitating the Personal and Spiritual workshops she developed. Among them 'Breathing Your Way to Peace', 'Tools for Moving Forward', and 'Building Self Esteem'. These days she truly loves facilitating 'Poetry Chat Box' and she will tell you how amazed she is by where the resulting discussions lead the participants.

Now she has donned the hat of an Author and Poet. A hat that suits her and sits well.

Patricia's long held desire to write a book became a reality when her first self-published book, Little Bit was published in 2020, followed by Willow's Dream in early 2021. Children and adults alike adore her books.

Though she admits to easily being distracted by taking time out to walk and indulge her passion for reading. She looks forward to seeing where her writing journey will take her.

Other works include:

Co-author in 'Colours of Me 'anthology (MMH press 2021)

Guest author in 'Law of Love' by K P Weaver (MMH press 2021)

'Little Bit' audio book (White Light Publishing)

'Little Bit' eBook Apple/Kobo

'Willow's Dream' eBook Barnes& Noble

Contributor to 'Inspire Knowledge' online magazine.

Little Bit – Winner of a Gold Award for New Age Non fiction and Silver Award for Inspirational MMH Press Awards

Both Little Bit and Willow's Dream hard and soft cover available through direct contact.

You can follow Patricia on the following links:

www.Facebook/Patricia Lovell author

www.Instagram/Patricia Lovell author